# FANNY FERN

## SELECTED WRITINGS

# FANNY FERN

## SELECTED WRITINGS

a *Broadview Anthology of American Literature* edition

Contributing Editor, *Fanny Fern: Selected Writings*:
Helena Snopek

General Editors, *The Broadview Anthology of American Literature*:

Derrick R. Spires, Cornell University
Rachel Greenwald Smith, Saint Louis University
Christina Roberts, Seattle University
Joseph Rezek, Boston University
Justine S. Murison, University of Illinois, Urbana-Champaign
Laura L. Mielke, University of Kansas
Christopher Looby, University of California, Los Angeles
Rodrigo Lazo, University of California, Irvine
Alisha Knight, Washington College
Hsuan L. Hsu, University of California, Davis
Michael Everton, Simon Fraser University
Christine Bold, University of Guelph

broadview press

BROADVIEW PRESS – www.broadviewpress.com
Peterborough, Ontario, Canada

Founded in 1985, Broadview Press remains a wholly independent publishing house. Broadview's focus is on academic publishing: our titles are accessible to university and college students as well as scholars and general readers. With over 800 titles in print, Broadview has become a leading international publisher in the humanities, with world-wide distribution. Broadview is committed to environmentally responsible publishing and fair business practices.

**Library and Archives Canada Cataloguing in Publication**

Title: Fanny Fern : selected writings / contributing editor, Fanny Fern: selected writings, Helena Snopek ; general editors, The Broadview anthology of American literature: Derrick R. Spires (Cornell University), Rachel Greenwald Smith (Saint Louis University), Christina Roberts (Seattle University), Joseph Rezek (Boston University), Justine S. Murison (University of Illinois, Urbana-Champaign), Laura L. Mielke (University of Kansas), Christopher Looby (University of California, Los Angeles), Rodrigo Lazo (University of California, Irvine), Alisha Knight (Washington College), Hsuan L. Hsu (University of California, Davis), Michael Everton (Simon Fraser University), Christine Bold (University of Guelph).
Other titles: Works. Selections
Names: Fern, Fanny, 1811-1872, author. | Snopek, Helena, editor. | Spires, Derrick Ramon, editor.
Description: Series statement: A Broadview anthology of American literature edition | Includes bibliographical references.
Identifiers: Canadiana (print) 20230223796 | Canadiana (ebook) 202302380X | ISBN 9781554816385 (softcover) | ISBN 9781770489004 (PDF) | ISBN 9781460408322 (EPUB)
Classification: LCC PS2523.P9 A6 2023 | DDC 813/.3—dc23

*Broadview Press handles its own distribution in North America:*
PO Box 1243, Peterborough, Ontario K9J 7H5, Canada
555 Riverwalk Parkway, Tonawanda, NY 14150, USA
Tel: (705) 743-8990; Fax: (705) 743-8353
email: customerservice@broadviewpress.com

For all territories outside of North America, distribution is handled by Eurospan Group.

Broadview Press acknowledges the financial support of the Government of Canada for our publishing activities.

Canada

Developmental Editor: Helena Snopek
Cover Designer: Lisa Brawn
Typesetter: Alexandria Stuart

PRINTED IN CANADA

# Contents

# Introduction

## Fanny Fern
## 1811 – 1872

Over the course of her twenty-year writing career, Fanny Fern became one of the most popular, well-paid, and influential prose writers of her era. Her work was simultaneously beloved by those who found her frank and often comedic observations on mid-nineteenth-century society entertaining and refreshing, and censured by those who found her style and subject matter—as well as her financial independence and determined professionalism—to be unbecoming in a woman. Fern's informal, conversational prose and regular use of colloquialisms marked an important shift in the established literary conventions of nineteenth-century fiction and journalism.

Fern was born Sara Payson Willis in Portland, Maine in 1811, to Nathaniel and Hannah Parker Willis. Her education was completed at the renowned Hartford Female Seminary run by educational reformer Catharine Beecher; over the course of her time at the school she developed a reputation both for her wild behavior and for her lively intelligence and interest in writing, which her father, a printer of religious books and newspapers, later put to use by engaging her as a proofreader.

In 1837, at the age of twenty-six, Fern married Boston banker Charles Eldredge; the couple had three daughters before Eldredge died in 1845. His death was the last in a year-long string of tragedies during which Fern also lost a sister, her mother, and the couple's eldest daughter. Eldredge, who had been engaged in an expensive lawsuit at the point of his death, left the family severely in debt. The financial support Fern received from her father and her in-laws was minimal and reluctantly given. Instead, she was pressed to follow the conventional path of remarriage, to which she eventually capitulated, marrying widower Samuel Farrington in 1849. The marriage was a disaster. Farrington was controlling, emotionally abusive, and wildly jealous; less than two years after their marriage, Fern scandalized both their families by leaving him. Farrington would later obtain a divorce on grounds of desertion.

Having lost all financial support from her family, Fern struggled to earn money for herself and her two daughters through taking in sewing work. Eventually, Fern started writing articles. She submitted a few to her brother Nathaniel Parker Willis, now a prominent magazine editor, but he refused to publish her work or to publicly associate himself with a sister he felt had shamed him. Two Boston newspapers, however—the *Olive Branch* and the *True Flag*—began accepting her articles in late 1851.

Fern's writings included both snappy satires and opinion pieces (many of which poked fun at contemporary marriage conventions and gender roles), as well as sentimental sketches about family, death, childhood, and religion; all were written in relaxed, conversational language that stood out from the more formal prose style popular at the time. The articles elicited substantial debate about the identity of their author, especially on the matter of gender. Many readers doubted that a woman could be capable of writing so indelicately, though others noted how many of her articles spoke intimately of "feminine" subjects. The articles proved exceptionally popular, so much so that they were regularly pirated in competing newspapers— including newspapers owned by Parker Willis.

By the summer of 1852, Fern—who had now established "Fanny Fern" as her pen name—was sufficiently popular to have been offered an exclusive contract with the New York *Musical World and Times*; she would spend the rest of her career in New York City. In 1853, Fern published her first book, *Fern Leaves from Fanny's Portfolio*, a collection of her articles. This collection emphasized Fern's more sentimental sketches—though her more acerbic and humorous opinion pieces were at least as well known and popular. The collection sold astonishingly well, both in the United States and Britain. Fern was celebrated for popularizing a new prose style that was at once lively, casual, and intimate; in an 1854 review of her work, *Harper's Magazine* enthusiastically wrote that "the day for stilted rhetoric, scholastic refinements, and big dictionary words, the parade and pomp and pageantry of literature, is declining."

Near the end of 1854, Fern published her first novel, *Ruth Hall: A Domestic Tale of the Present Time*. The work is heavily autobiographical, telling the rags-to-riches story of its eponymous heroine who is widowed as a young woman, falls into dire poverty, and, despite the censure of her family, establishes a lucrative career as a columnist. The novel was an overwhelming success—again, notwithstanding the vocal criticism of those who felt its tone, as well as its focus on an independent, enterprising woman, to be unfeminine. A large number of *Ruth Hall*'s characters were clearly drawn from real life, including the unsympathetic character Hyacinth Ellet, whom many in the literary community recognized to be an accurate portrait of Nathaniel Parker Willis. The revelation of Fern's true identity by a spiteful former publisher in December 1854 fueled the novel's popularity, though it also added to the condemnations of critics who felt that "a woman that unsexes herself to abuse her parents and relatives, however much they may deserve it, is not a very agreeable personage."

Fern was continually aggravated by critics' tendencies to evaluate the personalities and private lives of female writers more so than the merits or demerits of their writing. Nevertheless, she continued to write boldly over the following years, developing a reputation for addressing provocative topics such as prostitution and sexual mores, prison reform, labor and the gendered pay gap, women's legal rights, education and childcare, and more, as well as reviewing literature; she was notable for her unqualified praise of Walt Whitman's innovative and controversial *Leaves of Grass* in 1855.

In 1855, Fern was offered a contract with *The New York Ledger*, whose owner, Robert Bonner, proposed the astounding sum of $100 per article. Fern's work for the *Ledger* over the next decade-and-a-half contributed to its becoming one of the most popular and influential newspapers of its era. The following year, Fern married the writer James Parton, who had befriended her early in her time in New York. At a time when the earnings of married women could legally be claimed by their husbands, the couple negotiated marriage terms ensuring that Fern's earnings would remain hers alone, to be inherited by her own children upon her death. A second novel, *Rose Clark*, was published that same year; a subplot follows a character whose experiences with an abusive husband closely mirror Fern's own.

The remainder of Fern's career was dominated by her work for the *Ledger*, though she also continued to release collections of her articles (now with somewhat less of an emphasis on sentimental sketches). She died of cancer in 1872, having continued to write regularly until days before her death.

Despite her immense popularity and influence in the nineteenth century, Fern was largely dismissed by critics in the early twentieth. Many literary scholars, focusing on her sentimental sketches rather than her social commentary and satire, employed the same dismissive tone they used in discussing other "sentimental" women writers (such as Fern's friend, Frances Osgood); Fred Lewis Pattee infamously wrote, in his 1940 work of literary criticism *The Feminine Fifties*, that Fern was the "most tearful and convulsingly 'female' moralizer of the whole modern blue-stocking school." Today, a good deal of Fern's work strikes readers as both remarkably forward-thinking and refreshingly readable; twenty-first-century scholarship often focuses on understanding and reconciling the seeming dichotomies of Fern's work, which was by turns sentimental and satirical, conventional and ground-breaking.

## Note on the Texts

The versions of Fern's articles reprinted here are from the texts as they first appeared in her published collections, with four exceptions: the text of "Hints to Young Wives" is based on that which appeared in the 14 February 1852 issue of the *Olive Branch*, while the texts of "Male Criticism on Ladies' Books," "A Law More Nice than Just," and "Independence" are based on those that appeared in the *New York Ledger* in the 23 May 1857, the 10 July 1858, and the 30 July 1859 issues, respectively. The excerpts from *Ruth Hall: A Domestic Tale of the Present Time* are based on the text of the first edition, published in 1854. Spelling and punctuation have been modernized in accordance with the practices of *The Broadview Anthology of American Literature*.

CR

*Fanny Fern*
*Selected Writings*

# Hints to Young Wives

Shouldn't I like to make a bonfire of all the "Hints to Young Wives," "Married Woman's Friend," etc., and throw in the authors after them? I have a little neighbor who believes all they tell her is gospel truth, and lives up to it. The minute she sees her husband coming up the street, she makes for the door, as if she hadn't another minute to live, stands in the entry with her teeth chattering in her head till he gets all his coats and mufflers, and overshoes, and what-do-you-call-'ems off, then chases round (like a cat in a fit) after the boot-jack;[1] warms his slippers and puts 'em on, and dislocates her wrist carving at the table for fear it will tire him.

Poor little innocent fool! she imagines that's the way to preserve his affection. Preserve a fiddlestick! The consequence is, he's sick of the sight of her; snubs her when she asks him a question, and after he has eaten her good dinners takes himself off as soon as possible, bearing in mind the old proverb "that too much of a good thing is good for nothing." Now the truth is just this, and I wish all the women on earth had but one ear in common, so that I could put this little bit of gospel into it: Just so long as a man isn't quite as sure as if he knew for certain, whether nothing on earth could ever disturb your affection for him, he is your humble servant, but the very second he finds out (or thinks he does) that he has possession of every inch of your heart, and no neutral territory—he will turn on his heel and march off whistling "Yankee Doodle"!

Now it's no use to take your pocket handkerchief and go snivelling round the house with a pink nose and red eyes; not a bit of it! If you have made the interesting discovery that you were married for a sort of upper servant or housekeeper, just *fill that place and no other*, keep your temper, keep all his strings and buttons and straps on; and then keep him at a distance as a housekeeper should—"them's my sentiments!" I have seen one or two men in my life who could bear to be loved (as a woman with a soul knows how), without being spoiled by it, or converted into a tyrant—but they are rare birds, and should be

---

1  *boot-jack*  Tool used to assist in the removal of boots.

caught, stuffed and handed over to Barnum![1] Now as the ministers say, "I'll close with an interesting little incident that came under my observation."

Mr. Fern[2] came home one day when I had such a crucifying headache that I couldn't have told whether I was married or single, and threw an old coat into my lap to mend. Well, I tied a wet bandage over my forehead, "left all flying," and sat down to it—he might as well have asked me to make a *new* one; however I new lined the sleeves, mended the buttonholes, sewed on new buttons down the front, and all over the coat tails—when finally it occurred to me (I believe it was a suggestion of Satan) that the *pocket* might need mending; so I turned it inside out, and *what do you think I found?* A *love-letter from him to my dress-maker*!! I dropped the coat, I dropped the work-basket, I dropped the buttons, I dropped the baby (it was a *female*, and I thought it just as well to put her out of future misery) and then I hopped into a chair in front of the looking-glass, and remarked to the young woman I saw there, "*F-a-n-n-y F-e-r-n! if you—are—ever—such—a—confounded fool again*"—*and I wasn't.*
—1852

---

1    *Barnum*   Reference to the "American Museum" of entrepreneur P.T. Barnum (1810–91), which exhibited various scientific curiosities (many of which were hoaxes).

2    *Mr. Fern*   At the point at which this article was published, Fern was still legally married to the abusive Samuel Farrington, though she had left him early the previous year. Farrington eventually obtained a divorce on grounds of desertion.

# Thanksgiving Story

"Mary!" said the younger of two little girls, as they nestled under a coarse coverlid, one cold night in December, "tell me about Thanksgiving Day before papa went to heaven. I'm cold and hungry, and I can't go to sleep—I want something nice to think about."

"Hush!" said the elder child, "don't let dear mamma hear you; come nearer to me"; and they laid their cheeks together.

"I fancy papa was rich. We lived in a very nice house. I know there were pretty pictures on the wall; and there were nice velvet chairs, and the carpet was thick and soft, like the green moss-patches in the wood; and we had pretty goldfish on the side table, and Tony, my black nurse, used to feed them. And papa! you can't remember papa, Letty—he was tall and grand, like a prince, and when he smiled he made me think of angels. He brought me toys and sweetmeats, and carried me out to the stable, and set me on Romeo's live back, and laughed because I was afraid! And I used to watch to see him come up the street, and then run to the door to jump in his arms—he was a dear, kind papa," said the child, in a faltering voice.

"Don't cry," said the little one; "please tell me some more."

"Well, Thanksgiving day we were so happy; we sat around such a large table, with so many people—aunts and uncles and cousins—I can't think why they never come to see us now, Letty—and Betty made such sweet pies, and we had a big—big turkey; and papa would have me sit next to him, and gave me the wishbone, and all the plums out of his pudding; and after dinner he would take me in his lap, and tell me 'Red Riding Hood,' and call me 'pet,' and 'bird,' and 'fairy.' O, Letty, I can't tell any more; I believe I'm going to cry."

"I'm very cold," said Letty. "Does papa know, up in heaven, that we are poor and hungry now?"

"Yes—no—I can't tell," answered Mary, wiping away her tears; unable to reconcile her ideas of heaven with such a thought. "Hush! mamma will hear!"

Mamma had "heard." The coarse garment, upon which she had toiled since sunrise, dropped from her hands, and tears were forcing themselves, thick and fast, through her closed eyelids. The simple recital found but too sad an echo in that widowed heart.

—1853

# A Practical Bluestocking[1]

"Have you called on your old friend, James Lee, since your return?" said Mr. Seldon to his nephew.

"No, sir; I understand he has the misfortune to have a bluestocking for a wife, and whenever I have thought of going there, a vision with inky fingers, frowzled hair, rumpled dress, and slip-shod heels[2] has come between me and my old friend—not to mention thoughts of a disorderly house, smoky puddings,[3] and dirty-faced children. Defend me from a wife who spends her time dabbling in ink, and writing for the papers. I'll lay a wager James hasn't a shirt with a button on it, or a pair of stockings that is not full of holes. Such a glorious fellow as he used to be, too!" said Harry, soliloquizingly, "so dependent upon somebody to love him. By Jove, it's a hard case."

"Harry, will you oblige me by calling there?" said Mr. Seldon with a peculiar smile.

"Well, yes, if you desire it; but these married men get so metamorphosed by their wives, that it's a chance if I recognize the melancholy remains of my old friend. A literary wife!" and he shrugged his shoulders contemptuously.

At one o'clock the next afternoon, Harry might have been seen ringing the bell of James Lee's door. He had a very ungracious look upon his face, as much as to say—"My mind is made up for the worst, and I must bear it for Jemmy's sake."

The servant ushered him into a pretty little sitting room, not expensively furnished, but neat and tasteful. At the further end of the room were some flowering plants, among which a sweet-voiced canary was singing. Harry glanced round the room; a little light-stand or Chinese table stood in the corner, with pen, ink, and papers scattered over it.

"I knew it," said Harry; "there's the sign! horror of horrors! an untidy, slatternly bluestocking! how I shall be disgusted with her! Jemmy's to be pitied."

---

1   *Bluestocking* Literary or otherwise intellectually inclined woman, especially one who advocates for women's rights; the term often had a derogatory connotation in the nineteenth century.

2   *slip-shod heels* Shoes worn down at the heel, or otherwise poorly taken care of.

3   *smoky puddings* I.e., burnt desserts.

He took up a book that lay upon the table, and a little manuscript copy of verses fell from between the leaves. He dropped the book as if he had been poisoned; then picking up the fallen manuscript with his thumb and forefinger, he replaced it with an impatient pshaw! Then he glanced round the room again—no! there was not a particle of dust to be seen, even by his prejudiced eyes; the windows were transparently clean; the hearth-rug was longitudinally and mathematically laid down; the pictures hung "plumb" upon the wall; the curtains were fresh and gracefully looped; and, what was a greater marvel, there was a child's dress half finished in a dainty little work-basket, and a thimble of fairy dimensions in the immediate neighborhood thereof. Harry felt a perverse inclination to examine the stitches, but at the sound of approaching footsteps he braced himself up to undergo his mental shower-bath.

A little lady tripped lightly into the room, and stood smilingly before him; her glossy black hair was combed smoothly behind her ears, and knotted upon the back of a remarkably well-shaped head; her eyes were black and sparkling, and full of mirth; her dress fitted charmingly to a very charming little figure; her feet were unexceptionably small, and neatly gaitered;[1] the snowy fingers of her little hand had not the slightest "*soupçon*"[2] of ink upon them, as she extended them in token of welcome to her guest.

Harry felt very much like a culprit, and greatly inclined to drop on one knee, and make a clean breast of a confession, but his evil bachelor spirit whispered in his ear—"Wait a bit, she's fixed up for company; cloven foot[3] will peep out by and by!"

Well, they sat down! The lady knew enough—he heard that before he came; he only prayed that he might not be bored with her booklearning, or bluestockingism. It is hardly etiquette to report private conversations for the papers—so I will only say that when James Lee came home, two hours after, he found his old friend Harry in the finest possible spirits, *tête-à-tête*[4] with his "blue" wife. An invitation to dinner followed. Harry demurred—he had begun to look at the

---

1  *gaitered*   Covered with gaiters, cloth or leather coverings worn to protect shoes.
2  *soupçon*   French: tiny amount.
3  *cloven foot*   Sign of devilish intent.
4  *tête-à-tête*   In close conversation.

little lady through a very bewitching pair of spectacles, and he hated to be disenchanted—and a bluestocking dinner!

However, his objections, silent though they were, were overruled. There was no fault to be found with that tablecloth, or those snowy napkins; the glasses were clean, the silver bright as my lady's eyes; the meats cooked to a turn, the gravies and sauces perfect, and the dessert well got up and delicious. Mrs. Lee presided with ease and elegance; the custards and preserves were of her own manufacture, and the little prattler, who was introduced with them, fresh from her nursery bath, with moist ringlets, snowy robe, and dimpled shoulders, looked charmingly well cared for.

As soon as the two gentlemen were alone, Harry seized his friend's hand, saying, with a half smile, "James, I feel like an unmitigated scoundrel! I have heard your wife spoken of as a 'bluestocking,' and I came here prepared to pity you as the victim of an unshared heart, slatternly house, and indigestible cooking; but may I die an old bachelor if I don't wish that woman, who has just gone out, was my wife."

James Lee's eyes moistened with gratified pride. "You don't know half," said he. "Listen—some four years since[1] I became involved in business; at the same time my health failed me; my spirits were broken, and I was getting a discouraged man. Emma, unknown to me, made application as a writer to several papers and magazines. She soon became very popular; and not long after placed in my hands the sum of three hundred dollars, the product of her labor. During this time, no parental or household duty was neglected; and her cheerful and steady affection raised my drooping spirits, and gave me fresh courage to commence the world anew. She still continues to write, although, as you see, my head is above water. Thanks to her as my guardian angel, for she says, 'We must lay up something for a rainy day.' God bless her sunshiny face!"

The entrance of Emma put a stop to any further eulogy, and Harry took his leave in a very indescribable and penitential frame of mind, doing ample penance for his former unbelieving scruples, by being very uncomfortably in love with a "Bluestocking."

—1853

---

1 *since* Ago.

# Soliloquy of a Housemaid

Oh, dear, dear! Wonder if my mistress *ever* thinks I am made of flesh and blood! Five times, within half an hour, I have trotted upstairs, to hand her things, that were only four feet from her rocking chair. Then, there's her son, Mr. George—it does seem to me, that a great able-bodied man like him, needn't call a poor tired woman up four pair of stairs to ask "what's the time of day?" Heigho! it's "*Sally* do this," and "*Sally* do that," till I wish I never had been baptized at all; and I might as well go farther back, while I am about it, and wish I had never been born.

Now, instead of ordering me round so like a dray horse,[1] if they would only look up smiling-like, now and then; or ask me how my "rheumatiz"[2] did; or say good morning, Sally; or show some sort of interest in a fellow-cretur, I could pluck up a bit of heart to work for them. A kind word would ease the wheels of my treadmill amazingly, and wouldn't cost *them* anything, either.

Look at my clothes, all at sixes and sevens.[3] I can't get a minute to sew on a string or button, except at night; and then I'm so sleepy it is as much as ever I can find the way to bed; and what a bed it is, to be sure! Why, even the pigs are now and then allowed clean straw to sleep on; and as to bedclothes, the less said about them the better; my old cloak serves for a blanket, and the sheets are as thin as a charity school soup. Well, well; one wouldn't think it, to see all the fine glittering things down in the drawing-room. Master's span of horses, and Miss Clara's diamond earrings, and mistress's rich dresses. I *try* to think it is all right, but it is no use.

Tomorrow is Sunday—"day of *rest*," I believe they *call* it. H-u-m-p-h! more cooking to be done—more company—more confusion than on any other day in the week. If I own a soul I have not heard how to take care of it for many a long day. Wonder if my master and mistress calculate to pay me for *that*, if I lose it? It is a *question* in my mind. Land of Goshen! I ain't sure I've got a mind—there's the bell again!

—1853

---

1   *dray horse*   Work horse.
2   *rheumatiz*   Rheumatism.
3   *at sixes and sevens*   In disarray.

# Critics

Bilious wretches, who abuse you because you write better than they.

Slander and detraction! Even I, Fanny, know better than that. *I* never knew an editor to nib his pen with a knife as sharp as his temper, and write a scathing criticism on a book, because the author-ess had declined contributing to his paper. I never knew a man who had fitted himself to a promiscuous coat, cut out in a merry mood by taper fingers, to seize his porcupine quill, under the agony of too tight a *self-inflicted* fit, to annihilate the offender. I never saw the bottled-up hatred of years, concentrated in a single venomous paragraph. I never heard of an unsuccessful masculine author, whose books were drugs in the literary market, speak with a sneer of successful literary femininity, and insinuate that it was by *accident*, not *genius*, that they hit the popular favor!

By the memory of "seventy-six,"[1] No! Do you suppose a *man's* opinions are in the market—to be bought and sold to the highest bidder? Do you suppose he would laud a vapid book, because the fashionable authoress once laved his toadying[2] temples with the baptism of upper-tendom? or, do you suppose he'd lash a poor, but self-reliant wretch, who had presumed to climb to the topmost round of Fame's ladder, without *his* royal permission or assistance, and in despite of his repeated attempts to discourage her? No—no—bless your simple soul; a man never stoops to a meanness. There never was a criticism yet, born of envy, or malice, or repulsed love, or disappointed ambition. No—no. Thank the gods, *I* have a more exalted opinion of masculinity.

—1853

---

1  *seventy-six*   Idiomatic reference to 1776, the year of the signing of the Declaration of Independence.
2  *toadying*   Flattering.

# Mrs. Adolphus Smith Sporting the "Blue Stocking"

Well, I think I'll finish that story for the editor of the *Dutchman*. Let me see; where did I leave off? The setting sun was just gilding with his last ray—"Ma, I want some bread and molasses"—(yes, dear) gilding with his last ray the church spire—"Wife, where's my Sunday pants?" (*Under the bed, dear*) the church spire of Inverness, when a—"There's nothing under the bed, dear, but your lace cap"—(Perhaps they are in the coal hod in the closet) when a horseman was seen approaching—"Ma'am, the *pertators*[1] is out; not one for dinner"—(Take some turnips) approaching, covered with dust, and—"Wife! the baby has swallowed a button"—(*Reverse him*, dear—take him by the heels) and waving in his hand a banner, on which was written—"Ma! I've torn my pantaloons"—liberty or death! The inhabitants rushed *en masse*—"Wife! WILL you leave off scribbling?" (Don't be disagreeable, Smith, I'm just getting inspired) to the public square, where De Begnis, who had been secretly—"Butcher wants to see you, ma'am"—secretly informed of the traitors'—"Forgot *which* you said, ma'am, sausages or mutton chop"—movements, gave orders to fire; not less than twenty—"My gracious! Smith, you haven't been *reversing* that child all this time; he's as black as your coat; and that boy of YOURS has torn up the first sheet of my manuscript. There! it's no use for a married woman to cultivate her intellect—Smith, hand me those twins."

—1854

---

1  *pertators* Potatoes (the pronunciation of the word is meant to denote the typical speech habits of a servant).

# from *Ruth Hall: A Domestic Tale of the Present Time*

*Ruth Hall* (1854), Fanny Fern's first and most successful novel, is a heavily autobiographical account of an unconventional young woman named Ruth who rises from impoverished widowhood to wealth and celebrity as a newspaper columnist. The narrative begins with Ruth's marriage to the loving Harry Hall, who offers Ruth an escape from her unaffectionate family. The couple proceed to have three children—Daisy, Katy, and Nettie—though Daisy dies of croup early on. The subsequent death of Harry from typhoid fever leaves Ruth in desperate poverty, with neither her father nor her in-laws willing to provide her with sufficient financial support. After numerous fruitless attempts at finding employment—during which she is tricked into giving up her second daughter to be raised by the possessive and puritanically harsh Mr. and Mrs. Hall—Ruth finally finds financial success and personal fulfillment as a newspaper columnist (much as Fanny Fern herself had done). The novel ends with the reunion of Katy with her mother and younger sister, and with a word of encouragement from Mr. Walters, Ruth's publisher and friend, who tells her that "Life has much of harmony yet in store" for her.

*Sometimes* referred to as a *roman à clef*—a French term for a novel whose characters can often be directly identified with real-life figures—*Ruth Hall* includes a number of characters inspired by Fern's own family and experiences, including Ruth's brother Hyacinth Ellet, who has frequently been identified with Fern's brother, author Nathaniel Parker Willis.

## CHAPTER I

The old church clock rang solemnly out on the midnight air. Ruth started. For hours she had sat there, leaning her cheek upon her hand, and gazing through the open space between the rows of brick walls, upon the sparkling waters of the bay, glancing and quivering 'neath the moonbeams. The city's busy hum had long since died away; myriad restless eyes had closed in peaceful slumber; Ruth could not sleep. This was the last time she would sit at that little window. The morrow would find her in a home of her own. On the morrow Ruth would be a bride.

Ruth was not sighing because she was about to leave her father's roof (for her childhood had been anything but happy), but she was vainly trying to look into a future, which God has mercifully veiled from curious eyes. Had that craving heart of hers at length found its ark of refuge? Would clouds or sunshine, joy or sorrow, tears or smiles, predominate in her future? Who could tell? The silent stars returned her no answer. Would a harsh word ever fall from lips which now breathed only love? Would the step whose lightest footfall now made her heart leap, ever sound in her ear like a death-knell? As time, with its ceaseless changes, rolled on, would love flee affrighted from the bent form, and silver locks, and faltering footstep? Was there no talisman to keep him?

"Strange questions," were they, "for a young girl!" Ah, but Ruth could remember when she was no taller than a rosebush, how cravingly her little heart cried out for love! How a careless word, powerless to wound one less sensitive, would send her, weeping, to that little room for hours; and, young as she was, life's pains seemed already more to her than life's pleasures. Would it *always* be so? Would she find more thorns than roses in her *future* pathway?

Then, Ruth remembered how she used to wish she were beautiful—not that she might be admired, but that she might be loved. But Ruth was "very plain"—so her brother Hyacinth told her, and "awkward," too; she had heard that ever since she could remember; and the recollection of it dyed her cheek with blushes, whenever a stranger made his appearance in the home circle.

So, Ruth was fonder of being alone by herself; and then, they called her "odd," and "queer," and wondered if she would "ever make anything"; and Ruth used to wonder, too; and sometimes she asked herself why a sweet strain of music, or a fine passage in a poem, made her heart thrill, and her whole frame quiver with emotion?

The world smiled on her brother Hyacinth. He was handsome, and gifted. He could win fame, and what was better, love. Ruth wished he would love her a little. She often used to steal into his room and "right" his papers, when the stupid housemaid had displaced them; and often she would prepare him a tempting little lunch, and carry it to his room, on his return from his morning walk; but Hyacinth would only say, "Oh, it is you, Ruth, is it? I thought it was Bridget"; and go on reading his newspaper.

Ruth's mother was dead. Ruth did not remember a great deal about her—only that she always looked uneasy about the time her father was expected home; and when his step was heard in the hall, she would say in a whisper, to Hyacinth and herself, "Hush! hush! your father is coming"; and then Hyacinth would immediately stop whistling, or humming, and Ruth would run up into her little room, for fear she should, in some unexpected way, get into disgrace.

Ruth also remembered when her father came home and found company to tea, how he frowned and complained of headache, although he always ate as heartily as any of the company; and how after tea he would stretch himself out upon the sofa and say, "I think I'll take a nap"; and then, he would close his eyes, and if the company commenced talking, he would start up and say to Ruth, who was sitting very still in the corner, "*Ruth*, don't make such a noise"; and when Ruth's mother would whisper gently in his ear, "Wouldn't it be better, dear, if you laid down upstairs? it is quite comfortable and quiet there," her father would say, aloud, "Oh yes, oh yes, you want to get rid of me, do you?" And then her mother would say, turning to the company, "How very fond Mr. Ellet is of a joke!" But Ruth remembered that her mother often blushed when she said so, and that her laugh did not sound natural.

After her mother's death, Ruth was sent to boarding school, where she shared a room with four strange girls, who laid awake all night, telling the most extraordinary stories, and ridiculing Ruth for being such an old maid that she could not see "where the laugh came in." Equally astonishing to the unsophisticated Ruth was the demureness with which they would bend over their books when the pale, meek-eyed widow, employed as duenna,[1] went the rounds after tea, to see if each inmate was preparing the next day's lessons, and the coolness with which they would jump up, on her departure, put on their bonnets and shawls, and slip out at the side-street door to meet expectant lovers; and when the pale widow went the rounds again at nine o'clock, she would find them demurely seated, just where she left them, apparently busily conning[2] their lessons! Ruth wondered if *all* girls were as mischievous, and if fathers and mothers ever stopped to

---

1  *duenna*  Ladies' hired companion.
2  *conning*  Learning.

think what companions their daughters would have for roommates and bed-fellows, when they sent them away from home. As to the Principal, Madame Moreau, she contented herself with sweeping her flounces, once a day, through the recitation rooms; so it was not a difficult matter, in so large an establishment, to pass muster with the sub-teachers at recitations.

Composition day was the general bugbear. Ruth's madcap room-mates were struck with the most unqualified amazement and admiration at the facility with which "the old maid" executed this frightful task. They soon learned to put her services in requisition; first, to help them out of this slough of despond;[1] next, to save them the necessity of wading in at all, by writing their compositions for them.

In the all-absorbing love affairs which were constantly going on between the young ladies of Madame Moreau's school and their respective admirers, Ruth took no interest; and on the occasion of the unexpected reception of a bouquet, from a smitten swain,[2] accompanied by a copy of amatory verses, Ruth crimsoned to her temples and burst into tears, that anyone could be found so heartless as to burlesque the "awkward" Ruth. Simple child! She was unconscious that, in the freedom of that atmosphere where a "prophet out of his own country is honored,"[3] her lithe form had rounded into symmetry and grace, her slow step had become light and elastic, her eye bright, her smile winning, and her voice soft and melodious. Other bouquets, other notes, and glances of involuntary admiration from passers-by, at length opened her eyes to the fact, that she was "plain, awkward Ruth" no longer. Eureka! She had arrived at the first epoch in a young girl's life—she had found out her power! Her manners became assured and self-possessed. *She*, Ruth, could inspire love! Life became dear to her. There was something worth living for—something to look forward to. She had a motive—an aim; she should *some* day make somebody's heart glad—somebody's hearth-stone bright; somebody should be proud of her; and oh, how she *could* love that somebody! History,

---

1   *slough of despond*  Allusion to John Bunyan's popular Christian allegorical novel *The Pilgrim's Progress* (1678), in which the protagonist must make a trying journey through a swamp called the "Slough of Despond."

2   *swain*  Suitor.

3   *prophet out ... is honored*  See Mark 6.4: "But Jesus, said unto them, A prophet is not without honour, but in his own country, and among his own kin, and in his own house."

astronomy, mathematics, the languages, were all pastime now. Life wore a new aspect; the skies were bluer, the earth greener, the flowers more fragrant; her twin-soul existed somewhere.

When Ruth had been a year at school, her elegant brother Hyacinth came to see her. Ruth dashed down her books, and bounded down three stairs at a time to meet him; for she loved him, poor child, just as well as if he were worth loving. Hyacinth drew languidly back a dozen paces, and holding up his hands, drawled out imploringly, "kiss me if you insist on it, Ruth, but for heaven's sake, don't tumble my dickey."[1] He also remarked that her shoes were too large for her feet, and that her little French apron was "slightly askew"; and told her, whatever else she omitted, to be sure to learn "to waltz." He was then introduced to Madame Moreau, who remarked to Madame Chicchi, her Italian teacher, what a very *distingué*-looking person he was; after which he yawned several times, then touched his hat gracefully, praised "the very superior air of the establishment," brushed an imperceptible atom of dust from his beaver,[2] kissed the tips of his fingers to his demonstrative sister, and tiptoed Terpsichoreally[3] over the academic threshold.

In addition to this, Ruth's father wrote occasionally when a term-bill became due, or when his tradesmen's bills came in, on the first of January; on which occasion an annual fit of poverty seized him, an almshouse loomed up in perspective, he reduced the wages of his cook two shillings, and advised Ruth either to get married or teach school.

Three years had passed under Madame Moreau's roof; Ruth's schoolmates wondering the while why she took so much pains to bother her head with those stupid books, when she was every day growing prettier, and all the world knew that it was quite unnecessary for a pretty woman to be clever. When Ruth once more crossed the paternal threshold, Hyacinth levelled his eyeglass at her, and exclaimed, "'Pon honor, Ruth, you've positively had a narrow escape from being handsome." Whether old Mr. Ellet was satisfied with her physical and mental progress, Ruth had no means of knowing.

---

1   *tumble my dickey*  I.e., disturb my neatly arranged clothing. (A dickie was a stiff, false shirt front that was a standard part of male formal attire among the upper classes.)
2   *beaver*  I.e., beaver-fur hat.
3   *Terpsichoreally*  In a dance-like manner.

And now, as we have said before, it is the night before Ruth's bridal; and there she sits, though the old church bell has long since chimed the midnight hour, gazing at the moon, as she cuts a shining path through the waters; and trembling, while she questions the dim, uncertain future. Tears, Ruth? Have phantom shapes of terror glided before those gentle prophet eyes? Has death's dark wing even now fanned those girlish temples?

## CHAPTER 2

It was so odd in Ruth to have no one but the family at the wedding. It was just one of her queer freaks! Where was the use of her white satin dress and orange wreath? what the use of her looking handsomer than she ever did before, when there was nobody there to see her?

"Nobody to see her?" Mark[1] that manly form at her side; see his dark eye glisten, and his chiselled lip quiver, as he bends an earnest gaze on her who realizes all his boyhood dreams. Mistaken ones! it is not admiration which that young beating heart craves; it is love.

"A very fine-looking, presentable fellow," said Hyacinth, as the carriage rolled away with his new brother-in-law. "Really, love is a great beautifier. Ruth looked quite handsome tonight. Lord bless me! how immensely tiresome it must be to sit opposite the same face three times a day, three hundred and sixty-five days in a year! I should weary of Venus[2] herself. I'm glad my handsome brother-in-law is in such good circumstances. Duns[3] *are* a bore. I must keep on the right side of him. Tom, was that tailor here again yesterday? Did you tell him I was out of town? Right, Tom."

[In Chapter 3, Ruth moves in with her new husband, Harry Hall, and his strict mother.]

---

1   *Mark*   Notice.
2   *Venus*   Roman goddess of love and beauty.
3   *Duns*   Term usually referring to debt collectors, but in this case likely meaning people who are constantly asking for money.

## CHAPTER 4

"Good morning, Ruth; *Mrs. Hall* I suppose I *should* call you, only that I can't get used to being shoved one side quite so suddenly," said the old lady, with a faint attempt at a laugh.

"Oh, pray don't say Mrs. Hall to *me*," said Ruth, handing her a chair; "call me any name that best pleases you; I shall be quite satisfied."

"I suppose you feel quite lonesome when Harry is away, attending to business, and as if you hardly knew what to do with yourself; don't you?"

"Oh, no," said Ruth, with a glad smile, "not at all. I was just thinking whether I was not glad to have him gone a little while, so that I could sit down and think how much I love him."

The old lady moved uneasily in her chair. "I suppose you understand all about housekeeping, Ruth?"

Ruth blushed. "No," said she, "I have but just returned from boarding school. I asked Harry to wait till I had learned housekeeping matters, but he was not willing."

The old lady untied her cap strings, and patted the floor restlessly with her foot.

"It is a great pity you were not brought up properly," said she. "I learned all that a girl should learn, before I married. Harry has his fortune yet to make, you know. Young people, now-a-days, seem to think that money comes in showers, whenever it is wanted; that's a mistake; a penny at a time—that's the way we got ours; that's the way Harry and you will have to get yours. Harry has been brought up sensibly. He has been taught economy; he is, like me, naturally of a very generous turn; he will occasionally offer you pin-money.[1] In those cases, it will be best for you to pass it over to me to keep; of course you can always have it again, by telling me how you wish to spend it. I would advise you, too, to lay by all your handsome clothes. As to the silk stockings you were married in, of course you will never be so extravagant as to wear them again. I never had a pair of silk

---

1   *pin-money*   Allowance provided to a wife for her personal expenditure on clothing, household items, and other necessities.

stockings in my life; they have a very silly, frivolous look. Do you know how to iron, Ruth?"

"Yes," said Ruth; "I have sometimes clear-starched my own muslins and laces."

"Glad to hear it; did you ever seat[1] a pair of pantaloons?"

"No," said Ruth, repressing a laugh, and yet half inclined to cry; "you forget that I am just home from boarding school."

"Can you make bread? When I say *bread* I *mean* bread—old fashioned, yeast riz bread; none of your sal-soda, salæratus, sal-volatile poisonous mixtures,[2] that must be eaten as quick as baked, lest it should dry up; *yeast* bread—do you know how to make it?"

"No," said Ruth, with a growing sense of her utter good-for-nothingness; "people in the city always buy baker's bread; my father did."

"Your father! land's sake, child, you mustn't quote your father now you're married; you haven't any father."

I never had, thought Ruth.

"To be sure; what does the Bible say? 'Forsaking father and mother, cleave to your wife'[3] (or husband, which amounts to the same thing, I take it); and speaking of that, I hope you won't be always running home, or running anywhere in fact. Wives should be keepers at home. Ruth," continued the old lady after a short pause, "do you know I should like your looks better, if you didn't curl your hair?"

"I don't curl it," said Ruth, "it curls naturally."

"That's a pity," said the old lady, "you should avoid everything that looks frivolous; you must try and pomatum[4] it down. And Ruth, if you should feel the need of exercise, don't gad in the streets. Remember there is nothing like a broom and a dust-pan to make the blood circulate."

"You keep a rag bag,[5] I suppose," said the old lady; "many's the glass dish I've peddled away my scissors-clippings for. 'Waste not,

---

1  *seat*  I.e., repair the seat of.

2  *none of your ... poisonous mixtures*  Leavening agents such as baking powder were still relatively new developments in the 1850s, and many home cooks—especially those who lived in rural or less industrialized areas—held that breads leavened with such ingredients were vastly inferior to those leavened with yeast.

3  *Forsaking ... your wife*  See Genesis 2.24: "Therefore shall a man leave his father and his mother, and shall cleave unto his wife: and they shall be one flesh."

4  *pomatum*  Hair styling pomade.

5  *rag bag*  I.e., a bag containing scraps of fabric from sewing projects, which could be reused for various purposes such as mending tears or stuffing cushions.

want not.' I've got that framed somewhere. I'll hunt it up, and put it on your wall. It won't do you any harm to read it now and then.

"I hope," continued the old lady, "that you don't read novels and such trash. I have a very select little library, when you feel inclined to read, consisting of a treatise on 'The Complaints of Women,' an excellent sermon on Predestination,[1] by our old minister, Dr. Diggs, and Seven Reasons why John Rogers,[2] the martyr, must have had *ten* children instead of *nine* (as is *generally* supposed); any time that you stand in need of *rational* reading come to me"; and the old lady, smoothing a wrinkle in her black silk apron, took a dignified leave.

[In the intervening chapters, Ruth and Harry have their first child, named Daisy, and move into a home of their own.]

## CHAPTER 10

"You will be happy here, dear Ruth," said Harry; "you will be your own mistress."

Ruth danced about, from room to room, with the careless glee of a happy child, quite forgetful that she was a wife and a mother; quite unable to repress the flow of spirits consequent upon her newfound freedom.

Ruth's new house was about five miles from the city. The approach to it was through a lovely winding lane, a little off the main road, skirted on either side by a thick grove of linden and elms, where the wild grapevine leaped, clinging from branch to branch, festooning its ample clusters in prodigal profusion of fruitage, and forming a dense shade, impervious to the most garish noon-day heat; while beneath, the wild brier-rose unfolded its perfumed leaves in the hedges, till the bees and hummingbirds went reeling away, with their honeyed treasures.

You can scarce see the house for the drooping elms, half a century old, whose long branches, at every wind-gust, swept across the velvet

---

1  *Predestination*  Belief that the salvation or damnation of all human souls has already been predetermined by God, and is not dependent on the actions of individuals.
2  *John Rogers*  English clergy member (c. 1505–55), the first Protestant to be martyred by the Catholic queen Mary I, was burned at the stake.

lawn. The house is very old, but Ruth says, "All the better for that." Little patches of moss tuft the sloping roof, and swallows and martens twitter round the old chimney. It has nice old-fashioned beams running across the ceiling, which threaten to bump Harry's curly head. The doorways, too, are low, with honeysuckle, red and white, wreathed around the porches; and back of the house there is a high hill (which Ruth says must be terraced off for a garden), surmounted by a gray rock, crowned by a tumble-down old summer house, where you have as fine a prospect of hill and valley, rock and river, as ever a sunset flooded with rainbow tints.

It was blessed to see the love-light in Ruth's gentle eyes; to see the rose chase the lily from her cheek; to see the old spring come back to her step; to follow her from room to room, while she draped the pretty white curtains, and beautified, unconsciously, everything her fingers touched.

She could give an order without having it countermanded; she could kiss little Daisy without being called "silly"; she could pull out her comb, and let her curls flow about her face, without being considered "frivolous"; and, better than all, she could fly into her husband's arms, when he came home, and kiss him, without feeling that she had broken any penal statute. Yes; she was free as the golden orioles, whose hanging nests swayed to and fro amid the glossy green leaves beneath her window.

But not as thoughtless.

Ruth had a strong, earnest nature; she could not look upon this wealth of sea, sky, leaf, bud, and blossom; she could not listen to the little birds, nor inhale the perfumed breath of morning, without a filling eye and brimming heart, to the bounteous Giver. Should she revel in all this loveliness—should her heart be filled to its fullest capacity for earthly happiness, and no grateful incense go up from its altar to Heaven?

And the babe? Its wondering eyes had already begun to seek its mother's; its little lip to quiver at a harsh or discordant sound. An unpracticed hand must sweep that harp of a thousand strings;[1] trembling fingers must inscribe, indelibly, on that blank page, characters

---

1  *sweep that ... thousand strings*  Possible allusion to a verse of Hymn 19 by popular English hymnodist Isaac Watts (1674–1748): "Our life contains a thousand springs, / And dies if one be gone; / Strange, that a harp of thousand strings / Should keep in tune so long!"

to be read by the light of eternity: the maternal eye must never sleep at its post, lest the enemy rifle the casket of its gems. And so, by her child's cradle, Ruth first learned to pray. The weight her slender shoulders could not bear, she rolled at the foot of the cross; and, with the baptism of holy tears, mother and child were consecrated.

[In the ensuing chapters, Daisy dies of the croup, and Ruth and Harry subsequently have two more children, Katy and Nettie. Before long, Harry dies of the typhoid fever, leaving Ruth and their two young daughters in desperate poverty; Ruth's own relations provide her only minimal financial aid.]

## CHAPTER 56

It was a sultry morning in July. Ruth had risen early, for her cough seemed more troublesome in a reclining posture. "I wonder what that noise can be?" said she to herself; whir—whir—whir, it went, all day long in the attic overhead. She knew that Mrs. Waters had one other lodger beside herself, an elderly gentleman by the name of Bond, who cooked his own food, and whom she often met on the stairs, coming up with a pitcher of water, or a few eggs in a paper bag, or a pie that he had bought of Mr. Flake, at the little black grocery shop at the corner. On these occasions he always stepped aside, and with a deferential bow waited for Ruth to pass. He was a thin, spare man, slightly bent; his hair and whiskers curiously striped like a zebra, one lock being jet black, while the neighboring one was as distinct a white. His dress was plain, but very neat and tidy. He never seemed to have any business outdoors, as he stayed in his room all day, never leaving it at all till dark, when he paced up and down, with his hands behind him, before the house. "Whir—whir—whir." It was early sunrise; but Ruth had heard that odd noise for two hours at least. What *could* it mean? Just then a carrier passed on the other side of the street with the morning papers, and slipped one under the crack of the house door opposite.

A thought! why could not Ruth write for the papers? How very odd it had never occurred to her before! Yes, write for the papers— why not? She remembered that while at boarding school, an editor of a paper in the same town used often to come in and take down her compositions in shorthand as she read them aloud, and transfer them to the columns of his paper. She certainly *ought* to write better now than she did when an inexperienced girl. She would begin that very night; but where to make a beginning? who would publish her articles? how much would they pay her? to whom should she apply first? There was her brother Hyacinth, now the prosperous editor of the *Irving Magazine*; oh, if he would only employ her? Ruth was quite sure she could write as well as some of his correspondents, whom he had praised with no niggardly[1] pen. She would prepare samples to send immediately, announcing her intention, and offering them for his acceptance. This means of support would be so congenial, so absorbing. At the needle[2] one's mind could still be brooding over sorrowful thoughts.

Ruth counted the days and hours impatiently, as she waited for an answer. Hyacinth surely would not refuse *her* when in almost every number of his magazine he was announcing some new contributor; or, if *he* could not employ her *himself*, he surely would be brotherly enough to point out to her some one of the many avenues so accessible to a man of extensive newspaperial and literary acquaintance. She would so gladly support herself, so cheerfully toil day and night, if need be, could she only win an independence; and Ruth recalled with a sigh Katy's last visit to her father, and then she rose and walked the floor in her impatience; and then, her restless spirit urging her on to her fate, she went again to the post office to see if there were no letter. How long the clerk made her wait! Yes, there *was* a letter for her, and in her brother's handwriting too. Oh, how long since she had seen it!

Ruth heeded neither the jostling of office boys, porters, or draymen,[3] as she held out her eager hand for the letter. Thrusting it hastily in her pocket, she hurried in breathless haste back to her lodgings. The contents were as follows:

I have looked over the pieces you sent me, Ruth. It is very evident that writing never can be *your* forte; you have no talent that way. You may possibly be employed by some inferior newspapers, but be assured

---

1  *niggardly*  Stingy or begrudging.
2  *At the needle*  I.e., doing hand-sewing tasks for hire, a common but usually poorly paid means of support for unmarried or widowed women in the 1800s.
3  *draymen*  Cart drivers.

your articles never will be heard of out of your own little provincial city. For myself I have plenty of contributors, nor do I know of any of my literary acquaintances who would employ you. I would advise you, therefore, to seek some *unobtrusive* employment. Your brother,

Hyacinth Ellet

A bitter smile struggled with the hot tear that fell upon Ruth's cheek. "I have tried the unobtrusive employment," said Ruth; "the wages are six cents a day, Hyacinth"; and again the bitter smile disfigured her gentle lip.

"No talent!"

"At another tribunal than his will I appeal."

"Never be heard of out of my own little provincial city!" The cold, contemptuous tone stung her.

"But they shall be heard of"; and Ruth leaped to her feet. "Sooner than he dreams of, too. I *can* do it, I *feel* it, I *will* do it," and she closed her lips firmly; "but there will be a desperate struggle first," and she clasped her hands over her heart as if it had already commenced; "there will be scant meals, and sleepless nights, and weary days, and a throbbing brow, and an aching heart; there will be the chilling tone, the rude repulse; there will be ten backward steps to one forward. *Pride* must sleep! but—" and Ruth glanced at her children—"it shall be *done*. They shall be proud of their mother. *Hyacinth shall yet be proud to claim his sister.*"

"What is it, mamma?" asked Katy, looking wonderingly at the strange expression of her mother's face.

"What is it, my darling?" and Ruth caught up the child with convulsive energy; "what is it? only that when you are a woman you shall remember this day, my little pet"; and as she kissed Katy's upturned brow a bright spot burned on her cheek, and her eye glowed like a star.

[In the following chapter, the elder Mr. and Mrs. Hall—who have been seeking to gain custody of Ruth and Harry's children since their son's death—conspire to convince Ruth to give up Katy to their care. Desperate to be reunited with her elder daughter, Ruth intensifies her search for remunerative employment.]

## CHAPTER 59

"Is this *The Daily Type* office?" asked Ruth of a printer's boy, who was rushing down five steps at a time, with an empty pail in his hand.

"All you have to do is to ask, mem. You've got a tongue in your head, haven't ye? women folks generally has," said the little ruffian.

Ruth, obeying this civil invitation, knocked gently at the office door. A whir of machinery, and a bad odor of damp paper and cigar smoke, issued through the half-open crack.

"I shall have to walk in," said Ruth, "they never will hear my feeble knock amid all this racket and bustle"; and pushing the door ajar, she found herself in the midst of a group of smokers, who, in slippered feet, and with heels higher than their heads, were whiffing and laughing, amid the pauses of conversation, most uproariously. Ruth's face crimsoned as heels and cigars remained in *statu quo*,[1] and her glance was met by a rude stare.

"I called to see if you would like a new contributor to your paper," said Ruth; "if so, I will leave a few samples of my articles for your inspection."

"What do you say, Bill?" said the person addressed; "drawer full as usual, I suppose, isn't it? more chaff than wheat,[2] too, I'll swear; don't want any, ma'am; come now, Jo, let's hear the rest of that story; shut the door, ma'am, if you please."

"Are you the editor of the *Parental Guide?*" said Ruth, to a thin, cadaverous-looking gentleman, in a white neck-cloth, and green spectacles, whose editorial sanctum was not far from the office she had just left.

"I am."

"Do you employ contributors for your paper?"

"Sometimes."

"Shall I leave you this MS.[3] for your inspection, sir?"

"Just as you please."

---

1   *in statu quo*   Latin: in the same state. (I.e., the men did not lower their feet or stop smoking.)

2   *more chaff than wheat*   I.e., more poor-quality material than material worth publishing (the "chaff" is the husk of a grain of wheat).

3   *MS.*   Manuscript.

"Have you a copy of your paper here, sir, from which I could judge what style of articles you prefer?"

At this, the gentleman addressed raised his eyes for the first time, wheeled his editorial armchair round, facing Ruth, and peering over his green spectacles, remarked:

"Our paper, madam, is most em-phat-i-cal-ly a paper devoted to the interests of religion; no frivolous jests, no love-sick ditties, no fashionable sentimentalism, finds a place in its columns. This is a serious world, madam, and it ill becomes those who are born to die, to go dancing through it. Josephus remarks that the Saviour of the world was never known to smile.[1] *I* seldom smile. Are you a religious woman, madam?"

"I endeavor to become so," answered Ruth.

"V-e-r-y good; what sect?"

"Presbyterian."

At this the white neck-clothed gentleman moved back his chair: "Wrong, madam, all wrong; I was educated by the best of fathers, but he was *not* a Presbyterian; his son is not a Presbyterian; his son's paper sets its face like a flint against that heresy; no, madam, we shall have no occasion for your contributions; a hope built on a Presbyterian foundation, is built on the sand. Good morning, madam."

Did Ruth despair? No! but the weary little feet which for so many hours had kept pace with hers, needed a reprieve. Little Nettie must go home, and Ruth must read the office signs as she went along, to prepare for new attempts on the morrow.

Tomorrow? Would a brighter morrow *ever* come? Ruth thought of her children, and said again with a strong heart—*it will*; and taking little Nettie upon her lap she divided with her their frugal supper—a scanty bowl of bread and milk.

Ruth could not but acknowledge to herself that she had thus far met with but poor encouragement, but she knew that to climb, she must begin at the lowest round of the ladder. It were useless to apply to a long-established leading paper for employment, unless endorsed

---

1    *Josephus remarks ... to smile*   Reference to Roman Jewish historian Flavius Josephus (37–c. 100), whose *Antiquities of the Jews* contains two references to Jesus, both of which have often been taken as proof of Jesus' historical existence; the origin of the editor's comment about Jesus not smiling, however, is unclear.

by some influential name. Her brother had coolly, almost contemptuously, set her aside; and yet in the very last number of his Magazine, which accident threw in her way, he pleaded for public favor for a young actress, whom he said had been driven by fortune from the sheltered privacy of home, to earn her subsistence upon the stage, and whose earnest, strong-souled nature, he thought, should meet with a better welcome than mere curiosity. "Oh, why not one word for me?" thought Ruth; "and how can I ask of strangers a favor which a brother's heart has so coldly refused?"

It was very disagreeable applying to the small papers, many of the editors of which, accustomed to dealing with hoydenish[1] contributors, were incapable of comprehending that their manner towards Ruth had been marked by any want[2] of that respectful courtesy due to a dignified woman. From all such contact Ruth shrank sensitively; their free-and-easy tone fell upon her ear so painfully, as often to bring the tears to her eyes. Oh, if Harry—but she must not think of him.

The next day Ruth wandered about the business streets, looking into office entries, reading signs, and trying to gather from their "know-nothing"[3] hieroglyphics some light to illumine her darkened pathway. Day after day chronicled only repeated failures, and now, notwithstanding she had reduced their already meagre fare, her purse was nearly empty.

## from CHAPTER 62

Ruth had found employment. Ruth's MSS. had been accepted at the office of *The Standard*. Yes, an article of hers was to be published in the very next issue. The remuneration was not what Ruth had hoped, but it was at least a *beginning*, a stepping stone. What a pity that Mr. Lescom's (the editor's) rule was not to pay a contributor, even after a piece was accepted, until it was printed—and Ruth so short of funds.

---

1   *hoydenish*  Term applied to women perceived to be unmannered or otherwise unrespectable.
2   *want*  Lack.
3   *know-nothing*  Secretive; closed to outsiders. The reference is to the Know-Nothing Party, a nativist, strongly anti-immigration party that became prominent in American politics in the 1850s.

Could she hold out to work so hard, and fare so rigidly? for often there was only a crust left at night; but, God be thanked, she should now *earn* that crust! It was a pity that oil was so dear,[1] too, because most of her writing must be done at night, when Nettie's little prattling voice was hushed, and her innumerable little wants forgotten in sleep. Yes, it *was* a pity that good oil was so dear, for the cheaper kind crusted so soon on the wick, and Ruth's eyes, from excessive weeping, had become quite tender, and often very painful. Then it would be so mortifying should a mistake occur in one of her articles. She must write very legibly, for typesetters were sometimes sad bunglers, making people accountable for words that would set Worcester's or Webster's[2] hair on end; but, poor things, *they* worked hard too—they had *their* sorrows, thinking, long into the still night, as they scattered the types, more of their dependent wives and children, than of the orthography of a word, or the rhetoric of a sentence.

Scratch—scratch—scratch, went Ruth's pen; the dim lamp flickering in the night breeze, while the deep breathing of the little sleepers was the watchword, *On!* to her throbbing brow and weary fingers. One o'clock—two o'clock—three o'clock—the lamp burns low in the socket. Ruth lays down her pen, and pushing back the hair from her forehead, leans faint and exhausted against the windowsill, that the cool night-air may fan her heated temples. How impressive the stillness! Ruth can almost hear her own heart beat. She looks upward, and the watchful stars seem to her like the eyes of gentle friends. No, God would *not* forsake her! A sweet peace steals into her troubled heart, and the overtasked lids droop heavily over the weary eyes.

Ruth sleeps. ...

## Chapter 64

"I have good news for you," said Mr. Lescom to Ruth, at her next weekly visit; "your very first articles are copied, I see, into many of my exchanges, even into the ——, which seldom contains anything

---

1  *oil* I.e., to fuel an oil lamp;  *dear* Expensive.
2  *Worcester's or Webster's* Reference to what were then the two most prominent American dictionaries (founded respectively by lexicographers Joseph Emerson Worcester [1784–1865] and Noah Webster [1758–1843]).

but politics. A good sign for you, Mrs. Hall; a good test of your popularity."

Ruth's eyes sparkled, and her whole face glowed.

"Ladies *like* to be praised," said Mr. Lescom, good-humoredly, with a mischievous smile.

"Oh, it is not that—not that, sir," said Ruth, with a sudden moistening of the eye, "it is because it will be bread for my children."

Mr. Lescom checked his mirthful mood, and said, "Well, here is something good for me, too; a letter from Missouri, in which the writer says, that if 'Floy' (a pretty *nom-de-plume*[1] that of yours, Mrs. Hall) is to be a contributor for the coming year, I may put him down as a subscriber, as well as S. Jones, E. May, and J. Noyes, all of the same place. That's good news for *me*, you see," said Mr. Lescom, with one of his pleasant, beaming smiles.

"Yes," replied Ruth, abstractedly. She was wondering if her articles were to be the means of swelling Mr. Lescom's subscription list, whether *she* ought not to profit by it as well as himself, and whether she should not ask him to increase her pay. She pulled her gloves off and on, and finally mustered courage to clothe her thought in words.

"Now that's just *like* a woman," replied Mr. Lescom, turning it off with a joke; "give them the least foothold, and they will want the whole territory. Had I not shown you that letter, you would have been quite contented with your present pay. Ah! I see it won't do to talk so unprofessionally to you; and you needn't expect," said he, smiling, "that I shall ever speak of letters containing new subscribers on your account. I could easily get you the offer of a handsome salary by publishing such things. No—no, I have been foolish enough to lose two or three valuable contributors in that way; I have learned better than that, 'Floy'"; and taking out his purse, he paid Ruth the usual sum for her articles.

Ruth bowed courteously, and put the money in her purse; but she sighed as she went down the office stairs. Mr. Lescom's view of the case was a business one, undoubtedly; and the same view that almost any other business man would have taken, *viz*.:[2] to retain her at her present low rate of compensation, till he was necessitated to raise it by

---

1   *nom-de-plume*  French: pen name.
2   *viz*.  Latin: namely; that is to say.

a higher bid from a rival quarter. And so she must plod wearily on till that time came, and poor Katy must still be an exile; for she had not enough to feed her, her landlady having raised the rent of her room two shillings, and Ruth being unable to find cheaper accommodations. It *was* hard, but what could be done? Ruth believed she had exhausted all the offices she knew of. Oh! there was one, *The Pilgrim*; she had not tried there. She would call at the office on her way home.

The editor of *The Pilgrim* talked largely. He had, now, plenty of contributors; he didn't know about employing a new one. Had she ever written? and *what* had she written? Ruth showed him her article in the last number of *The Standard*.

"Oh—hum—hum!" said Mr. Tibbetts, changing his tone; "so you are 'Floy,' are you?" (casting his eyes on her). "What pay do they give you over there?"

Ruth was a novice in business matters, but she had strong common sense, and that common sense said, he has no right to ask you that question; don't you tell him; so she replied with dignity, "My bargain, sir, with Mr. Lescom, was a private one, I believe."

"Hum," said the foiled Mr. Tibbetts; adding in an undertone to his partner, "sharp that!"

"Well, if I conclude to engage you," said Mr. Tibbetts, "I should prefer you would write for me over a different signature than the one by which your pieces are indicated at *The Standard* office, or you can write exclusively for my paper."

"With regard to your first proposal," said Ruth, "if I have gained any reputation by my first efforts, it appears to me that I should be foolish to throw it away by the adoption of another signature; and with regard to the last, I have no objection to writing exclusively for you, if you will make it worth my while."

"Sharp again," whispered Tibbetts to his partner.

The two editors then withdrawing into a further corner of the office, a whispered consultation followed, during which Ruth heard the words, "Can't afford it, Tom; hang it! we are head over ears in debt now to that paper man; good articles though—deuced good—must have her if we dispense with some of our other contributors. We had better begin low though, as to terms, for she'll go up now like a rocket, and when she finds out her value we shall have to increase her pay, you know."

(Thank you, gentlemen, thought Ruth, when the cards change hands, I'll take care to return the compliment.)

In pursuance of Mr. Tibbetts' shrewd resolution, he made known his "exclusive" terms to Ruth, which were no advance upon her present rate of pay at *The Standard*. This offer being declined, they made her another, in which, since she would not consent to do otherwise, they agreed she should write over her old signature, "Floy," furnishing them with two articles a week.

Ruth accepted the terms, poor as they were, because she could at present do no better, and because every pebble serves to swell the current.

Months passed away while Ruth hoped and toiled, "Floy's" fame as a writer increasing much faster than her remuneration. There was rent-room to pay, little shoes and stockings to buy, oil, paper, pens, and ink to find; and now autumn had come, she could not write with stiffened fingers, and wood and coal were ruinously high, so that even with this new addition to her labor, Ruth seemed to retrograde pecuniarily, instead of advancing; and Katy still away! She must work harder—harder. Good, brave little Katy; she, too, was bearing and hoping on—mamma had promised, if she would stay there, patiently, she would certainly take her away just as soon as she had earned money enough; and mamma *never* broke her promise—*never*; and Katy prayed to God every night, with childish trust, to help her mother to earn money, that she might soon go home again.

And so, while Ruth scribbled away in her garret, the public were busying themselves in conjecturing who "Floy" might be. Letters poured in upon Mr. Lescom with their inquiries, even bribing him with the offer to procure a certain number of subscribers, if he would divulge her real name; to all of which the old man, true to his promise to Ruth, to keep her secret inviolate, turned a deaf ear. All sorts of rumors became rife about "Floy," some maintaining her to be a man, because she had the courage to call things by their right names, and the independence to express herself boldly on subjects which to the timid and clique-serving were tabooed. Some said she was a disappointed old maid; some said she was a designing[1] widow; some said

---

[1] *designing* Plotting (i.e., to obtain a husband).

she was a moon-struck girl; and all said she was a nondescript.[1] Some tried to imitate her, and failing in this, abused and maligned her; the outwardly strait-laced and inwardly corrupt puckered up their mouths and "blushed for her"; the hypocritical denounced the sacrilegious fingers which had dared to touch the Ark;[2] the fashionist voted her a vulgar, plebeian thing; and the earnest and sorrowing, to whose burdened hearts she had given voice, cried God speed her. And still "Floy" scribbled on, thinking only of bread for her children, laughing and crying behind her mask—laughing all the more when her heart was heaviest; but of this her readers knew little and would have cared less. Still her little bark breasted the billows,[3] now rising high on the topmost wave, now merged in the shadows, but still steering with straining sides, and a heart of oak, for the nearing port of Independence.

Ruth's brother, Hyacinth, saw "Floy's" articles floating through his exchanges with marked dissatisfaction and uneasiness. That she should have succeeded in any degree without his assistance was a puzzle, and the premonitory symptoms of her popularity, which his weekly exchanges furnished, in the shape of commendatory notices, were gall and wormwood[4] to him. *Something* must be done, and that immediately. Seizing his pen, he dispatched a letter to Mrs. Millet, which he requested her to read to Ruth, alluding very contemptuously to Ruth's articles, and begging her to use her influence with Ruth to desist from scribbling, and seek some other employment. *What* employment, he did not condescend to state; in fact, it was a matter of entire indifference to him, provided she did not cross his track. Ruth listened to the contents of the letter, with the old bitter smile, and went on writing.

---

1   *nondescript*   Person of unremarkable appearance.
2   *sacrilegious fingers ... the Ark*   Reference to the Old Testament story of Uzzah, who is struck down and killed by God after disobeying the divine commandment not to touch the Ark of the Covenant; see 2 Samuel 6.3–8 and 1 Chronicles 13.7–11.
3   *bark breasted the billows*   Ship rode the waves.
4   *were gall and wormwood*   Evoked feelings of bitterness; *gall* Bile; *wormwood* Bitter herb, toxic in large amounts.

## from Chapter 65

Pushing aside her papers, she discovered two unopened letters which Mr. Lescom had handed her, and which she had, in the hurry of finishing her next article, quite forgotten. Breaking the seal of the first, she read as follows:

To "Floy."

I am a rough old man, Miss, and not used to writing or talking to ladies. I don't know who you are, and I don't ask; but I take *The Standard*, and I like your pieces. I have a family of bouncing girls and boys; and when we've all done work, we get round the fire of an evening, while one of us reads your pieces aloud. It may not make much difference to you what an old man thinks, but I tell you those pieces have got the real stuff in 'em, and so I told my son John the other night; and *he* says, and *I* say, and neighbor Smith, who comes in to hear 'em, says, that you ought to make a book of them, so that your readers may keep them. You can put me down for three copies, to begin with; and if every subscriber to *The Standard* feels as I do, you might make a plum[1] by the operation. Suppose, now, you think of it?

N.B.—John says, maybe you'll be offended at my writing to you, but I say you've got too much common sense.

Yours to command,

John Stokes

"Well, well," said Ruth, laughing, "that's a thought that never entered this busy head of mine, John Stokes. *I* publish a book? Why, John, are you aware that those articles were written for bread and butter, not fame; and tossed to the printer before the ink was dry, or I had time for a second reading? And yet, perhaps, there is more freshness about them than there would have been, had I leisure to have pruned and polished them—who knows? I'll put your suggestion on file, friend Stokes, to be turned over at my leisure. It strikes me, though, that it will keep awhile. Thank you, honest John. It is just such readers as you whom I like to secure. Well, what have we here?" and Ruth broke the seal of the second letter. It was in a delicate, beautiful, female hand; just such a one as you, dear Reader, might trace,

---

1  *make a plum*  Earn a large amount of money.

whose sweet, soft eyes, and long, drooping tresses, are now bending over this page. It said:

Dear "Floy":

For you *are* "dear" to me, dear as a sister on whose loving breast I have leaned, though I never saw your face. I know not whether you are young and fair, or old and wrinkled, but I know that your heart is fresh, and guileless, and warm as childhood's; and that every week your printed words come to me, in my sick chamber, like the ministrations of some gentle friend, sometimes stirring to its very depths the fountain of tears, sometimes, by odd and quaint conceits, provoking the mirthful smile. But "Floy," I love you best in your serious moods; for as earth recedes, and eternity draws near, it is the real and tangible my soul yearns after. And sure I am, "Floy," that I am not mistaken in thinking that we both lean on the same Rock of Ages; both discern, through the mists and clouds of time, the Sun of Righteousness.[1] I shall never see you, "Floy," on earth; mysterious voices, audible only to the dying ear, are calling me away; and yet, before I go, I would send you this token of my love, for all the sweet and soul-strengthening words you have unconsciously sent to my sick chamber, to wing the weary, waiting hours. We shall *meet*, "Floy"; but it will be where "tears are wiped away."[2]

God bless you, my unknown sister.

Mary R——

Ruth's head bowed low upon the table, and her lips moved; but He to whom the secrets of all hearts are known, alone heard that grateful prayer.

---

1  *Rock of Ages*  Allusion to the popular Christian hymn of the same name written by Augustus Toplady in 1763, in which the "Rock of Ages," a sheltering cave, serves as a metaphor for Jesus Christ;  *the Sun of Righteousness*  See Malachi 4.2: "But unto you that fear my name shall the Sun of righteousness arise with healing in his wings; and ye shall go forth, and grow up as calves of the stall."

2  *where "tears are wiped away"*  Allusion to the description of Heaven given in Revelation 21.4: "And God shall wipe away all tears from their eyes; and there shall be no more death, neither sorrow, nor crying, neither shall there be any more pain: for the former things are passed away."

## from CHAPTER 72

The first letter Ruth opened on her return, was a request from a Professor of some College for her autograph for himself and some friends; the second, an offer of marriage from a Southerner, who confessed to one hundred negroes,[1] "but hoped that the strength and ardor of the attachment with which the perusal of her articles had inspired him, would be deemed sufficient atonement for this in her Northern eyes. The frozen North," he said, "had no claim on such a nature as hers; the sunny South, the land of magnolias and orange blossoms, the land of love, *should* be her chosen home. Would she not smile on him? She should have a box at the opera, a carriage, and servants in livery, and the whole heart and soul of Victor Le Pont."

The next was more interesting. It was an offer to "Floy" from a publishing house, to collect her newspaper articles into a volume. They offered to give her so much on a copy, or $800 for the copyright. An answer was requested immediately. In the same mail came another letter of the same kind from a distant State, also offering to publish a volume of her articles.

"Well, well," soliloquized Ruth, "business is accumulating. I don't see but I shall have to make a book in spite of myself; and yet those articles were written under such disadvantages, would it be *wise* in me to publish so soon? But Katy? and $800 copyright money?" Ruth glanced round her miserable, dark room, and at the little stereotyped[2] bowl of bread and milk that stood waiting on the table for her supper and Nettie's; $800 *copyright money*! it *was* a temptation; but supposing her book should prove a hit? and bring double, treble, fourfold that sum, to go into her publisher's pockets instead of hers? how provoking! Ruth straightened up, and putting on a very resolute air, said, "No, gentlemen, I will *not* sell you my copyright; these autograph letters, and all the other letters of friendship, love, and business, I am constantly receiving from strangers, are so many proofs that I have won the public ear. No, I will not sell my copyright; I will rather deny myself a while longer, and accept the percentage"; and so she sat down and wrote her publishers; but then caution whispered, what if

---

1    *to one hundred negroes* I.e., to owning one hundred enslaved people.
2    *stereotyped* I.e., recurring over and over again. (The term "stereotype" originally referred to the metal plates used in the printing process to create identical copies of printed materials.)

her book should *not* sell? "Oh, pshaw," said Ruth, "it *shall!*" and she brought her little fist down on the table till the old stone inkstand seemed to rattle out "*it shall!*" ...

## Chapter 74

Those of my readers who are well acquainted with journalism know that some of our newspapers, nominally edited by the persons whose names appear as responsible in that capacity, *seldom*, perhaps *never*, contain an article from their pen, the whole paper being "made up" by some obscure individual, with more brains than pennies, whose brilliant paragraphs, metaphysical essays, and racy book reviews are attributed (and tacitly fathered) by the comfortably fed gentlemen who keep these, their factotums,[1] in some garret, just one degree above starving point. In the city, where board is expensive, and single gentlemen are "taken in and done for," under many a sloping attic roof are born thoughts which should win for their originators fame and independence.

Mr. Horace Gates, a gentlemanly, slender, scholar-like-looking person, held this nondescript and unrecognized relation to the *Irving Magazine*; the nominal editor, Ruth's brother Hyacinth, furnishing but one article a week, to deduct from the immense amount of labor necessary to their weekly issue.

"Heigho," said Mr. Gates, dashing down his pen; "four columns yet to make up; I am getting tired of this drudgery. My friend Seaten told me that he was dining at a restaurant the other day, when my employer, Mr. Hyacinth Ellet, came in, and that a gentleman took occasion to say to Mr. E., how much he admired *his* article in the last *Irving Magazine*, on 'City Life.' *His* article! it took me one of the hottest days this season, in this furnace of a garret, with the beaded drops standing on my suffering forehead, to write that article, which, by the way, has been copied far and wide.[2] His article! and the best of the joke is (Seaten says) the cool way in which Ellet thanked him, and pocketed all the credit of it! But what's this? here's a note from the very gentleman himself:

---

1   *factotums*   Employees who do all manner of work.
2   *copied far and wide*   I.e., reprinted in other newspapers, a common practice of nineteenth-century journalism.

Mr. Gates;

Sir—I have noticed that you have several times scissorized from the exchanges articles over the signature of 'Floy,' and inserted them in our paper. It is my wish that all articles bearing that signature should be excluded from our paper, and that no allusion be made to her, in any way or shape, in the columns of the *Irving Magazine*. As you are in our business confidence, I may say that the writer is a sister of mine, and that it would annoy and mortify me exceedingly to have the fact known; and it is my express wish that you should not, hereafter, in any way, aid in circulating her articles.

Yours, etc.,

Hyacinth Ellet

"What does that mean?" said Gates; "*his* sister? why don't he want her to write? I have cut out every article of hers as fast as they appeared; confounded good they are, too, and I call myself a judge; they are better, at any rate, than half our paper is filled with. This is all very odd—it stimulates my curiosity amazingly—*his* sister? married or unmarried, maid, wife, or widow? She can't be poor when he's so well off (gave $100 for a vase which struck his fancy yesterday, at Martini's). I don't understand it. 'Annoy and mortify him exceedingly'; what *can* he mean? I must get at the bottom of that; she is becoming very popular, at any rate; her pieces are traveling all over the country—and here is one, to my mind, as good as anything *he* ever wrote. Ha! ha! perhaps that's the very idea now—perhaps he wants to be the only genius in the family. Let him! if he can; if she don't win an enviable name, and in a very short time too, I shall be mistaken. I wish I knew something about her. Hyacinth is a heartless dog—pays me principally in fine speeches; and because I am not in a position just now to speak my mind about it. I suppose he takes me for the pliant tool I appear. By Jupiter! it makes my blood boil; but let me get another and better offer, Mr. Ellet, and see how long I will write articles for you to father, in this confounded hot garret. '*His* sister!' I will inquire into that. I'll bet a box of cigars she writes for daily bread—Heaven help her, if she does, poor thing!— it's hard enough, as I know, for a *man* to be jostled and snubbed round in printing offices. Well, well, it's no use wondering, I must go to work; what a pile of books here is to be reviewed! wonder who reads all the books? Here is *Uncle Sam's Log House*. Mr. Ellet writes me that I must simply announce the book without comment, for fear of offending southern subscribers. The word 'slave' I know has been tabooed in our columns this long while, for the same reason.[1] Here are poems by Lina Lintney—weak as diluted water, but the authoress once paid Mr. Ellet a compliment in a newspaper article, and here is her 'reward of merit' (in a memorandum attached to the book, and just sent down by Mr. Ellet); 'give this volume a first-rate notice.' Bah! what's the use of criticism when a man's opinion can be bought and sold that way? it is an imposition on the public. There is *The Barolds* too; I am to 'give that a capital notice,' because the authoress introduced Mr. Ellet into fashionable society when a young man. The grammar in that book would give Lindley Murray convulsions, and the construction of the sentences drive Blair[2] to a mad-house. Well, a great deal [of] the dear public know what a book is, by the reviews of it in this paper. Heaven forgive me the lies I tell this way on compulsion.

"The humbuggery of this establishment is only equalled by the gullibility of the dear public. Once a month, now, I am ordered to puff[3] every 'influential paper in the Union,' to ward off attacks on the *Irving Magazine*, and the bait takes, too, by Jove. That little *Tea-Table Tri-Mountain Mercury* has not muttered or peeped about Hyacinth's 'toadyism[4] when abroad,' since Mr. Ellet gave me orders to praise 'the typographical and literary excellence of that widely circulated paper.' Then, there is the editor of *The Bugbear*, a cut-and-thrust-bludgeon-pen-and-ink-desperado, who makes the mincing,[5] aristocratic Hyacinth quake in his patent-leather boots. I have orders to toss him a sugar-plum occasionally, to keep his plebeian mouth shut; something after the French maxim, 'always to praise a

---

1   *Uncle Sam's Log House … reason*   Thinly veiled reference to Harriet Beecher Stowe's *Uncle Tom's Cabin* (1852), which was extremely popular in Northern states but vilified by many Southern whites.

2   *Lindley Murray*   American grammarian (1745–1826) whose books were widely used in American and English schools;   *Blair*   Scottish Enlightenment theologian and philosopher Hugh Blair (1718–1800).

3   *puff*   Praise (especially in a publishing context), often with the implication of the praise being overblown or unmerited.

4   *toadyism*   Self-interested servility.

5   *mincing*   Affectedly refined.

person for what they *are not*'—for instance, 'our very *gentlemanly* neighbor and contemporary, the discriminating and refined editor of *The Bugbear*, whose very readable and spicy paper,' etc., etc. Then there is the *religious* press. Hyacinth, having rather a damaged reputation, is anxious to enlist them on his side, particularly the editor of *The Religious Platform*. I am to copy at least one of his editorials once a fortnight, or in some way call attention to his paper. Then, if Hyacinth chooses to puff actresses, and call Mme. —— a 'splendid personation of womanhood,' and praise her equivocal writings in his paper, which lies on many a family table to be read by innocent young girls, he knows the caustic pen of that religious editor will never be dipped in ink to reprove him. That is the way it is done. Mutual admiration-society—bah! I wish *I* had a paper. Wouldn't I call things by their right names? Would I know any sex in books? Would I praise a book because a woman wrote it? Would I abuse it for the same reason? Would I say, as one of our most able editors said not long since to his reviewer, 'cut it up root and branch; what right have these women to set themselves up for authors, and reap literary laurels?' Would I unfairly insert all the adverse notices of a book, and never copy one in its praise? Would I pass over the wholesale swindling of some aristocratic scoundrel, and trumpet in my police report, with heartless comments, the name of some poor, tempted, starving wretch, far less deserving of censure, in God's eye, than myself? Would I have my tongue or my pen tied in any way by policy, or interest, or clique-ism? No—sir! The world never will see a paper till mine is started. Would I write long descriptions of the wardrobe of foreign *prima donnas*, who bring their cracked voices and reputations to our American market, and 'occupy suites of rooms lined with satin, and damask, and velvet,' and goodness knows what, and give their reception-soirees, at which they '*affably notice*' our toadying first citizens? By Jupiter! why *shouldn't* they be 'affable'? Don't they come over here for our money and patronage? Who cares how many 'bracelets' Signora —— had on, or whose 'arm she leaned gracefully upon,' or whether her 'hair was braided or curled'? If, because a lord or a duke once 'honored her' by insulting her with infamous proposals, some few brainless Americans choose to deify her as a goddess, in the name of George Washington and common sense, let it not be taken as a national exponent. There are some few Americans left, who prefer ipecac in homœopathic doses."[1]

## CHAPTER 75

"Hark![2] Nettie. Go to the door, dear," said Ruth, "someone knocked."

"It is a strange gentleman, mamma," whispered Nettie, "and he wants to see you."

Ruth bowed as the stranger entered. She could not recollect that she had ever seen him before, but he looked very knowing, and, what was very provoking, seemed to enjoy her embarrassment hugely. He regarded Nettie, too, with a very scrutinizing look, and seemed to devour everything with the first glance of his keen, searching eye. He even seemed to listen to the whir—whir—whir of the odd strange lodger in the garret overhead.

"I don't recollect you," said Ruth, hesitating, and blushing slightly; "you have the advantage of me, sir?"

"And yet you and I have been writing to each other for a week or more," replied the gentleman, with a good-humored smile; "you have even signed a contract, entitling me to your pen-and-ink services."

"Mr. Walter?" said Ruth, holding out her hand.

"Yes," replied Mr. Walter, "I had business this way, and I could not come here without finding you out."

"Oh, thank you," said Ruth, "I was just wishing that I had some head wiser than mine, to help me decide on a business matter which came up two or three days ago. Somehow I don't feel the least reluctance to bore you with it, or a doubt that your advice will not be just the thing; but I shall not stop to dissect the philosophy of that feeling, lest in grasping at the shadow, I should lose the substance," said she, smiling.

While Ruth was talking, Mr. Walter's keen eye glanced about the room, noting its general comfortless appearance, and the little bowl of bread and milk that stood waiting for their supper. Ruth observed this, and blushed deeply. When she looked again at Mr. Walter, his eyes were glistening with tears.

"Come here, my darling," said he to Nettie, trying to hide his emotion.

---

1  *ipecac* Unpleasant substance that, in small doses, had only modest effects, but that in larger doses would induce vomiting;  *homœopathic doses* Small doses.

2  *Hark* Listen.

"I don't know you," answered Nettie.

"But you will, my dear, because I am your mamma's friend."

"Are you Katy's friend?" asked Nettie.

"Katy?" repeated Mr. Walter.

"Yes, my *sister* Katy; she can't live here, because we don't have supper enough; pretty soon mamma will earn more supper, won't you, mamma? Shan't you be glad when Katy comes home, and we all have enough to eat?" said the child to Mr. Walter.

Mr. Walter pressed his lips to the child's forehead with a low "Yes, my darling," and then placed his watch chain and seals at her disposal, fearing Ruth might be painfully affected by her artless prattle.

Ruth then produced the different publishers' offers she had received for her book, and handed them to Mr. Walter.

"Well," said he, with a gratified smile, "I am not at all surprised; but what are you going to reply?"

"Here is my answer," said Ruth, "*i.e.*, provided your judgment endorses it. I am a novice in such matters, you know, but I cannot help thinking, Mr. Walter, that my book will be a success. You will see that I have acted upon that impression, and refused to sell my copyright."

"You don't approve it?" said she, looking a little confused, as Mr. Walter bent his keen eyes on her, without replying.

"But I do though," said he; "I was only thinking how excellent a substitute strong common sense may be for experience. Your answer is brief, concise, sagacious, and business-like; I endorse it unhesitatingly. It is just what I should have advised you to write. You are correct in thinking that your book will be popular, and wise in keeping the copyright in your own hands. In how incredibly short a time you have gained a literary reputation, Floy."

"Yes," answered Ruth, smiling, "it is all like a dream to me"; and then the smile faded away, and she shuddered involuntarily as the recollection of all her struggles and sufferings came vividly up to her remembrance.

Swiftly the hours fled away as Mr. Walter, with a brother's freedom,[1] questioned Ruth as to her past life and drew from her the details of her eventful history.

---

1  *freedom*  I.e., familiarity; openness.

"Thank God, the morning dawneth," said he in a subdued tone, as he pressed Ruth's hand, and bade her a parting goodnight.

Ruth closed the door upon Mr. Walter's retreating figure, and sat down to peruse the following letters, which had been sent her to Mr. Walter's care, at the *Household Messenger* office.

Mrs. or Miss "Floy":

Permit me to address you on a subject which lies near my heart, which is, in fact, a subject of pecuniary importance to the person now addressing you. My story is to me a painful one; it would doubtless interest you; were it written and published, it would be a thrilling tale.

Some months since[1] I had a lover whom I adored, and who said he adored me. But as Shakespeare has said, "The course of true love never did run smooth":[2] ours soon became an uphill affair; my lover proved false, ceased his visits, and sat on the other side of the meeting house.[3] On my writing to him and desiring an explanation, he insultingly replied that I was not what his fancy had painted me. Was that *my* fault? false, fickle, ungenerous man! But I was not thus to be deceived and shuffled off. No; I employed the best counsel in the State and commenced an action for damages, determined to get some balm for my wounded feelings; but owing to the premature death of my principal witness, I lost the case and the costs were heavy. The excitement and worry of the trial brought on a fever, and I found myself, on my recovery, five hundred dollars in debt; I intend to pay every cent of this, but how am I to pay it? My salary for teaching school is small and it will take me many years. I want you, therefore, to assist me by writing out my story and giving me the book. I will furnish all the facts, and the story, written out by your magic pen, would be a certain success. A publisher in this city has agreed to publish it for me if you will write it. I could then triumph over the villain who so basely deceived me.

Please send me an early answer, as the publisher referred to is in a great hurry.

Very respectfully yours,

Sarah Jarmesin

---

1   *since*   Ago.
2   *The course ... run smooth*   See Shakespeare's *A Midsummer Night's Dream* 1.1.136.
3   *meeting house*   Church.

"Well," said Ruth, laughing, "my bump of invention will be entirely useless, if my kind friends keep on furnishing me with subjects at this rate. Here is letter No. 2."

Dear "Floy":

My dog Fido is dead. He was a splendid Newfoundland, black and shaggy; father gave $10 for him when he was a pup. We all loved him dearly. He was a prime dog, could swim like a fish. The other morning we found him lying motionless on the doorstep. Somebody had poisoned poor Fido. I cried all that day, and didn't play marbles for a whole week. He is buried in the garden, and I want you to write an epithalamium[1] about him. My brother John, who is looking over my shoulder, is laughing like everything; he says 't is an epitaph, not an epithalamium that I want, just as if *I* didn't know what I want? John is just home from college, and thinks he knows everything. It is my dog, and I'll fix his tombstone just as I like. Fellows in round jackets[2] are not always fools. Send it along quick, please, "Floy"; the stone-cutter is at work now. What a funny way they cut marble, don't they? (With sand and water.) Johnny Weld and I go there every recess, to see how they get on with the tombstone. Don't stick in any Latin or Greek, now, in your epithalamium. Our John cannot call for a glass of water without lugging in one or the other of them; I'm sick as death of it. I wonder if I shall be such a fool when I go to college. You ought to be glad you are a woman, and don't have to go. Don't forget Fido, now. Remember, he was six years old, black, shaggy, with a white spot on his forehead, and rather a short-ish tail—a prime dog, I tell *you*.

Billy Sands

"It is a harrowing case, Billy," said Ruth, "but I shall have to let Fido pass; now for letter No. 3."

Dear Madam:

I address a stranger, and yet *not* a stranger, for I have read your heart in the pages of your books. In these I see sympathy for the poor, the sorrowing, and the dependent; I see a tender love for helpless childhood.

---

1  *epithalamium*  Wedding song.
2  *round jackets*  Also known as *roundabouts*, short, tight-fitting jackets often worn by young schoolboys during this period.

Dear "Floy," I am an orphan, and that most wretched of all beings, a loving, but unloved wife. The hour so dreaded by all maternity draws near to me. It has been revealed to me in dreams that I shall not survive it. "Floy," will you be a mother to my babe? I cannot tell you why I put this trust in one whom I have only known through her writings, but something assures me it will be safe with you; that you only can fill my place in the little heart that this moment is pulsating beneath my own. Oh, do not refuse me. There are none in the wide world to dispute the claim I would thus transfer to you. Its father—but of him I will not speak; the wine cup is my rival. Write me speedily. I shall die content if your arms receive my babe.

Yours affectionately,

Mary Andrews

"Poor Mary! that letter must be answered," said Ruth, with a sigh; "ah, here is one more letter."

Miss, or Mrs., or Madam Floy:

I suppose by this time you have become so inflated that the honest truth would be rather unpalatable to you; nevertheless, I am going to send you a few plain words. The rest of the world flatters you—I shall do no such thing. You have written tolerably, all things considered, but you violate all established rules of composition, and are as lawless and erratic as a comet. You may startle and dazzle, but you are fit only to throw people out of their orbits. Now and then, there's a gleam of something like reason in your writings, but for the most part they are unmitigated trash—false in sentiment—unrhetorical in expression; in short, were you my daughter, which I thank a good Providence you are not, I should box your ears, and keep you on a bread and water diet till you improved. That you *can* do better, if you will, I am very sure, and that is why I take the pains to find fault, and tell you what none of your fawning friends will.

You are not a genius—no, madam, not by many removes; Shakespeare was a genius—Milton[1] was a genius—the author of *History of the Dark Ages*, which has reached its fifteenth edition, was a genius (you may not know you have now the honor of being addressed by him); no, madam, you are not a genius, nor have I yet seen a just criticism of your writings; they are all either over-praised, or

---

[1]  *Milton*  English poet John Milton, known especially for his epic poem *Paradise Lost* (1667).

over-abused; you have a certain sort of talent, and that talent, I grant you, is peculiar; but a genius—no, no, Mrs., or Miss, or Madam Floy—you don't approach genius, though I am not without a hope that, if you are not spoiled by injudicious, sycophantic admirers, you may yet produce something creditable; although I candidly confess, that it is my opinion, that the *female* mind is incapable of producing anything which may be strictly termed *literature*.

Your honest friend,

William Stearns

Prof. of Greek, Hebrew, and Mathematics, in Hopetown College, and author of *History of the Dark Ages*.

"Oh vanity! thy name is William Stearns," said Ruth.

## CHAPTER 77

And now our heroine had become a regular business woman. She did not even hear the whir—whir of the odd lodger in the attic. The little room was littered with newspapers, envelopes, letters opened and unopened, answered and waiting to be answered. One minute she might be seen sitting, pen in hand, trying, with knit brows, to decipher some horrible cabalistic[1] printer's mark on the margin of her proof; then writing an article for Mr. Walter, then scribbling a business letter to her publishers, stopping occasionally to administer a sedative to Nettie, in the shape of a timely quotation from Mother Goose,[2] or to heal a fracture in a doll's leg or arm. Now she was washing a little soiled face, or smoothing little rumpled ringlets, replacing a missing shoestring or pinafore button, then wading through the streets while Boreas[3] contested stoutly for her umbrella, with parcels and letters to the post-office (for Ruth must be her own servant), regardless of gutters or thermometers, regardless of jostling or crowding. What cared she for all these, when Katy would soon be back—poor little patient, suffering Katy? Ruth felt as if wings were growing from her shoulders. She never was weary, or sleepy, or hungry. She had not the slightest idea, till long after, what an

---

1   *cabalistic*   Mysterious; undecipherable.
2   *Mother Goose*   Fictional narrator of a number of English folk tales and nursery rhymes.
3   *Boreas*   Mythological personification of the north wind.

incredible amount of labor she accomplished, or how her *mother's heart* was goading her on.

"Pressing business that Miss Hall must have," said her landlady, with a sneer, as Ruth stood her dripping umbrella in the kitchen sink. "Pressing business, running round to offices and the like of that, in such a storm as this. You wouldn't catch *me* doing it if I was a widder.[1] I hope I'd have more regard for appearances. I don't understand all this flying in and out, one minute up in her room, the next in the street, forty times a day, and letters by the wholesale. It will take me to inquire into it. It may be all right, hope it is; but of course I like to know what is going on in my house. This Miss Hall is so terrible close-mouthed, I don't like it. I've thought a dozen times I'd like to ask her right straight out who and what she is, and done with it; but I have not forgotten that little matter about the pills,[2] and when I see her, there's something about her, she's civil enough too, that seems to say, 'don't you cross that chalk-mark, Sally Waters.' I never had lodgers afore like her and that old Bond, up in the garret. They are as much alike as two peas. *She* goes scratch—scratch—scratch; *he* goes whir—whir—whir. They haint spoke a word to one another since that child was sick. It's enough to drive anybody mad, to have such a mystery in the house. I can't make head nor tail on't. John, now, he don't care a rush-light about it; no more he wouldn't, if the top of the house was to blow off; but there's nothing plagues *me* like it, and yet I ain't a bit curous nuther. Well, neither she nor Bond make me any trouble, there's that in it; if they did I wouldn't stand it. And as long as they both pay their bills so reg'lar, I shan't make a fuss; I *should* like to know though what Miss Hall is about all the time."

———

Publication day came at last. There was *the* book. Ruth's book! Oh, how few of its readers, if it were fortunate enough to find readers, would know how much of her own heart's history was there laid bare. Yes, there was the book. She could recall the circumstances under which each separate article was written. Little shoeless feet were covered with the proceeds of this; a little medicine, or a warmer shawl,

---

1   *widder*   Widow.

2   *that little ... pills*   In a previous chapter, Ruth had offended her landlady by refusing an offer of some unnamed pills after she had exhibited a bad cough, probably brought on by the unhealthy conditions of her lodging.

was bought with that. This was written, faint and fasting, late into the long night; that composed while walking wearily to or from the offices where she was employed. One was written with little Nettie sleeping in her lap; another still, a mirthful, merry piece, as an escape-valve for a wretched heartache. Each had its own little history. Each would serve, in after-days, for a landmark to some thorny path of bygone trouble. Oh, if the sun of prosperity, after all, should gild these rugged paths! Some virtues—many faults—the book had—but God speed it, for little Katy's sake!

"Let me see, please," said little Nettie, attracted by the gilt covers, as she reached out her hand for the book.

"Did you make those pretty pictures, mamma?"

"No, my dear—a gentleman, an artist, made those for me—*I* make pictures with a-b-c's."

"Show me one of your pictures, mamma," said Nettie.

Ruth took the child upon her lap, and read her the story of Gertrude. Nettie listened with her clear eyes fixed upon her mother's face.

"Don't make her die—oh, please don't make her die, mamma," exclaimed the sensitive child, laying her little hand over her mother's mouth.

Ruth smiled, and improvised a favorable termination to her story, more suitable to her tender-hearted audience.

"That is nice," said Nettie, kissing her mother; "when I get to be a woman shall I write books, mamma?"

"God forbid," murmured Ruth, kissing the child's changeful cheek; "God forbid," murmured she, musingly, as she turned over the leaves of her book; "no happy woman ever writes. From Harry's grave sprang 'Floy.'"

## CHAPTER 87

"Good morning, Mr. Ellet!" said Mr. Jones, making an attempt at a bow, which the stiffness of his shirt-collar rendered entirely abortive;[1] "how d'ye do?"

"Oh, how are you, Mr. Jones? I was just looking over the *Household Messenger* here, reading my daughter 'Floy's' pieces, and thinking

---

1    *abortive*   Self-defeating; pointless.

what a great thing it is for a child to have a good father. 'Floy' was carefully brought up and instructed, and this, you see, is the result. I have been reading several of her pieces to a clergyman, who was in here just now. I keep them on hand in my pocket-book, to exhibit as a proof of what early parental education and guidance may do in developing latent talent, and giving the mind a right direction."

"I was not aware 'Floy' *was* your daughter," replied Mr. Jones; "do you know what time she commenced writing? what was the title of her first article and what was her remuneration?"

"Sir?" said Mr. Ellet, wishing to gain a little time, and looking very confused.

"Perhaps I should not ask such questions," said the innocent Mr. Jones, mistaking the cause of Mr. Ellet's hesitation; "but I felt a little curiosity to know something of her early progress. What a strong desire you must have felt for her ultimate success; and how much your influence and sympathy must have assisted her. Do you know whether her remuneration at the commencement of her career as a writer, was above the ordinary average of pay?"

"Yes—no—really, Mr. Jones, I will not venture to say, lest I should make a mistake; my memory is apt to be so treacherous."

"She wrote merely for amusement, I suppose; there could be no *necessity* in *your* daughter's case," said the blundering Mr. Jones.

"Certainly not," replied Mr. Ellet.

"It is astonishing how she can write so feelingly about the poor," said Mr. Jones; "it is so seldom that an author succeeds in depicting truthfully those scenes for which he draws solely upon the imagination."

"My daughter, 'Floy,' has a very vivid imagination," replied Mr. Ellet, nervously. "Women generally have, I believe; they are said to excel our sex in word-painting."

"I don't know but it may be so," said Jones. "'Floy' certainly possesses it in an uncommon degree. It is difficult else to imagine, as I said before, how a person, who has always been surrounded with comfort and luxury, could describe so feelingly the other side of the picture. It is remarkable. Do you know how much she has realized by her writings?"

"There, again," said the disturbed Mr. Ellet, "my memory is at fault; I am not good at statistics."

"Some thousands, I suppose," replied Mr. Jones. "Well, how true it is, that 'to him who hath shall be given!'[1] Now, here is your literary daughter, who has no need of money, realizes a fortune by her books, while many a destitute and talented writer starves on a crust."

"Yes," replied Mr. Ellet, "the ways of Providence are inscrutable."

—1854

---

1   *to him ... be given!*   See Mark 4.25.

# from Fern's *New York Ledger* review of Walt Whitman's *Leaves of Grass*

Well baptized: fresh, hardy, and grown for the masses. Not more welcome is their natural type to the winter-bound, bed-ridden, and spring-emancipated invalid. "Leaves of Grass" thou art unspeakably delicious, after the forced, stiff, Parnassian exotics[1] for which our admiration has been vainly challenged.

Walt Whitman, the effeminate world needed thee. The timidest soul whose wings ever drooped with discouragement, could not choose but rise on thy strong pinions.

> Undrape—you are not guilty to me, nor stale nor discarded;
> I see through the broadcloth and gingham whether or no.[2]

· · · · · · · · · ·

> O despairer, here is my neck,
> You shall *not* go down! Hang your whole weight upon me.[3]

Walt Whitman, the world needed a "Native American" of thorough, out and out breed—enamored of *women* not *ladies*, *men* not *gentlemen*; something beside a mere Catholic-hating Know-Nothing;[4] it needed a man who dared speak out his strong, honest thoughts, in the face of pusillanimous, toadying,[5] republican aristocracy; dictionary-men, hypocrites, cliques and creeds; it needed a large-hearted, untainted, self-reliant, fearless son of the Stars and

---

1   *Parnassian exotics*   Poets overly indebted to formal, European poetic traditions; later in the century the term often referred to a group of poets who rejected the informality and perceived sentimentality of Romantic poetry, though it is unlikely that Fern intends that specific meaning here.

2   *Undrape ... whether or no*   See lines 137–38 of the poem later titled "Song of Myself."

3   *O despairer ... upon me*   See lines 1007–08 of the poem later titled "Song of Myself."

4   *Catholic-hating Know-Nothing*   Fern refers to the nativist political party the Know Nothings, formally known as the Native American Party, known for their anti-immigrant, anti-Catholic stance.

5   *toadying*   Inclined to flattery.

Stripes, who disdains to sell his birthright for a mess of pottage;[1] who does

Not call one greater or one smaller,
That which fills its period and place being equal to any;[2]

who will

Accept nothing which all cannot have their counterpart of on the same terms.[3]

Fresh "Leaves of Grass!" not submitted by the self-reliant author to the fingering of any publisher's critic,[4] to be arranged, re-arranged and disarranged to his circumscribed liking, till they hung limp, tame, spiritless, and scentless. No. It were a spectacle worth seeing, this glorious Native American, who, when the daily labor of chisel and plane was over, himself, with toil-hardened fingers, handled the types to print the pages which wise and good men have since delighted to endorse and to honor. Small critics, whose contracted vision could see no beauty, strength, or grace, in these "Leaves," have long ago repented that they so hastily wrote themselves down shallow by such a premature confession. Where an Emerson, and a Howitt[5] have commended, my woman's voice of praise may not avail; but happiness was born a twin, and so I would fain share with others the unmingled delight which these "Leaves" have given me.

I say unmingled; I am not unaware that the charge of coarseness and sensuality has been affixed to them. My moral constitution may

---

1 *sell his ... of pottage*  I.e., to exchange something valuable for something immediately desirable but not of intrinsic or lasting value. The idiom refers to the biblical story of Esau, who sells his birthright to his brother Jacob in exchange for a bowl of lentil stew; see Genesis 25.29–34.

2 *Not call ... to any*  See lines 1142–43 of the poem later titled "Song of Myself."

3 *Accept nothing ... same terms*  See line 508 of the poem later titled "Song of Myself."

4 *not submitted ... publisher's critic*  Whitman self-published the first edition of *Leaves of Grass*, and was also responsible for much of its typesetting.

5 *Emerson*  Transcendental philosopher, lecturer, and poet Ralph Waldo Emerson (1803–82), one of the most prominent public intellectuals in nineteenth-century America, whose private commendations of *Leaves of Grass* became widely known throughout the literary community; *Howitt*  English writer William Howitt (1792–1879); his positive review of *Leaves of Grass* was published in *The London Weekly Dispatch* on 9 March 1856.

be hopelessly tainted or—too sound to be tainted, as the critic wills, but I confess that I extract no poison from these "Leaves"—to me they have brought only healing. Let him who can do so, shroud the eyes of the nursing babe lest it should see its mother's breast. Let him look carefully between the gilded covers of books, backed by high-sounding names, and endorsed by parson and priest, lying unrebuked upon his own family table; where the asp[1] of sensuality lies coiled amid rhetorical flowers. Let him examine well the paper dropped weekly at his door, in which virtue and religion are rendered disgusting, save when they walk in satin slippers, or, clothed in purple and fine linen, kneel on a damask *"prie-dieu."*[2]

Sensual!—No—the moral assassin looks you not boldly in the eye by broad daylight; but Borgia-like[3] takes you treacherously by the hand, while from the glittering ring on his finger he distils through your veins the subtle and deadly poison.

Sensual? The artist who would inflame, paints you not nude Nature, but stealing Virtue's veil, with artful artlessness now conceals, now exposes, the ripe and swelling proportions.

Sensual? Let him who would affix this stigma upon "Leaves of Grass," write upon his heart, in letters of fire, these noble words of its author:

> In woman I see the bearer of the great fruit, which is immortality • • • •
> the good thereof is not tasted by *roues*, and never can be.[4] ...

[Fern here includes a number of further quotations from Whitman's text.]

I close the extracts from these "Leaves," which it were easy to multiply, for one is more puzzled what to leave unculled, than what to gather, with the following sentiments; for which, and for all the good

---

1    *asp*   Poisonous snake.

2    *clothed in purple*   Reference to the historical association of purple fabrics with royalty;   *prie-dieu*   Table for prayer, often highly ornamental.

3    *Borgia-like*   Reference to the House of Borgia, a Spanish royal family who came to political and ecclesiastical prominence during the fifteenth century, and whose members were involved in numerous political scandals and intrigues.

4    *In woman ... can be*   Slight misquotation from the 1855 version of the poem eventually titled "I Sing the Body Electric";   *roues*   Libertines; sexually licentious men.

things included between the covers of his book, Mr. Whitman will please accept the cordial grasp of a woman's hand:

The wife—and she is not one jot less than the husband,
The daughter—and she is just as good as the son,
The mother—and she is every bit as much as the father.[1]

FANNY FERN

—1856

---

1   *The wife … the father*   Lines from the poem eventually titled "A Song for Occupations."

# Male Criticism on Ladies' Books

> Courtship and marriage, servants and children, these are the great objects of a woman's thoughts, and they necessarily form the staple topics of their writings and their conversation. We have no right to expect anything else in a woman's book.—*N.Y. Times*

Is it in feminine novels *only* that courtship, marriage, servants and children are the staple? Is not this true of all novels? Of Dickens, of Thackeray, of Bulwer[1] and a host of others? Is it peculiar to feminine pens, most astute and liberal of critics? Would a novel be a novel if it did not treat of courtship and marriage? and if it could be so recognized, would it find readers? When I see such a narrow, snarling criticism as the above, I always say to myself, the writer is some unhappy man, who has come up without the refining influence of mother, or sister, or reputable female friends; who has divided his migratory life between boarding houses, restaurants, and the outskirts of editorial sanctums; and who knows as much about reviewing a woman's book, as I do about navigating a ship, or engineering an omnibus[2] from the South Ferry, through Broadway, to Union Park. I think I see him writing that paragraph in a fit of spleen[3]—of *male* spleen—in his small boarding house upper chamber, by the cheerful light of a solitary candle, flickering alternately on cobwebbed walls, dusty washstand, begrimed bowl and pitcher, refuse cigar stumps, boot-jacks,[4] old hats, buttonless coats, muddy trousers, and all the wretched accompaniments of solitary, selfish male existence, not to speak of his own puckered, unkissable face; perhaps, in addition, his boots hurt, his cravat-bow persists in slipping under his ear for want[5] of a pin, and a wife to pin it (poor wretch!), or he has been refused by some pretty girl, as he deserved to be (narrow-minded old vinegar-cruet![6]), or snubbed by some lady authoress; or, more trying than all to the male constitution, has had a weak cup of coffee for that morning's breakfast.

---

1   *Dickens ... Bulwer*   Three popular male nineteenth-century novelists: Charles Dickens (1812–70), William Makepeace Thackeray (1811–63), and Edward Bulwer-Lytton (1803–73).
2   *omnibus*   Horse-drawn public carriage traveling a fixed route with set stops.
3   *spleen*   Bad temper.
4   *boot-jacks*   Implements to assist in the removal of boots.
5   *want*   Lack.
6   *cruet*   Bottle.

But seriously—we have had quite enough of this shallow criticism (?) on lady-books. Whether the book which called forth the remark above quoted was a good book or a bad one, I know not: I should be inclined to think the *former* from the dispraise of such a pen. Whether ladies can write novels or not, is a question I do not intend to discuss; but that some of them have no difficulty in finding either publishers or readers is a matter of history; and that gentlemen often write over feminine signatures would seem also to argue that feminine litera-ture is, after all, in good odor[1] with the reading public. Granted that lady-novels are not all that they should be—is such shallow, unfair, wholesome, sneering criticism (?) the way to reform them? Would it not be better and more manly to point out a better way kindly, justly, *and, above all, respectfully*? or—what would be a much harder task for such critics—write a better book!

—1857

---

1   *odor*  Favor.

# A Law More Nice[1] than Just

Here I have been sitting twiddling the morning paper between my fingers this half hour, reflecting upon the following paragraph in it: "Emma Wilson was arrested yesterday for wearing man's apparel."[2] Now, why this should be an actionable offense is past my finding out, or where's the harm in it, I am as much at a loss to see. Think of the old maids (and weep) who have to stay at home evening after evening, when, if they provided themselves with a coat, pants and hat, they might go abroad, instead of sitting there with their noses flattened against the window-pane, looking vainly for "the Coming Man."[3] Think of the married women who stay at home after their day's toil is done, waiting wearily for their thoughtless, truant husbands, when they might be taking the much needed independent walk in trousers, which custom forbids to petticoats. And this, I fancy, may be the secret of this famous law—who knows? It *wouldn't* be pleasant for some of them to be surprised by a touch on the shoulder from some dapper young fellow, whose familiar treble voice belied his corduroys. That's it, now. What a fool I was not to think of it—not to remember that men who make the laws, make them to meet all these little emergencies.

Everybody knows what an everlasting drizzle of rain we have had lately, but nobody but a woman, and a woman who lives on fresh air and outdoor exercise, knows the thraldom of taking her daily walk through a three weeks' rain, with skirts to hold up, and umbrella to hold down, and puddles to skip over, and gutters to walk round, and all the time in a fright lest, in an unguarded moment, her calves should become visible to some one of those rainy-day philanthropists who are interested in the public study of female anatomy.

One evening, after a long rainy day of scribbling, when my nerves were in double-twisted knots, and I felt as if myriads of little ants were leisurely traveling over me, and all for want of the walk which is my daily salvation, I stood at the window, looking at the slanting, persistent

---

1   *Nice*   Proper; overly invested in the appearance of propriety.
2   *Emma Wilson ... man's apparel*   In the mid-to-late nineteenth century, many American municipalities had bylaws prohibiting individuals from dressing in garments conventionally associated with the opposite sex.
3   *the Coming Man*   I.e., a promising suitor.

rain, and took my resolve. "*I'll do it*," said I, audibly, planting my slipper upon the carpet. "Do what?" asked Mr. Fern,[1] looking up from a big book. "Put on a suit of your clothes and take a tramp with you," was the answer. "You dare not," was the rejoinder; "you are a little coward, only saucy on paper." It was the work of a moment, with such a challenge, to fly upstairs and overhaul my philosopher's wardrobe. Of course we had fun. Tailors[2] must be a stingy set, I remarked, to be so sparing of their cloth, as I struggled into a pair of their handiwork, undeterred by the vociferous laughter of the wretch who had solemnly vowed to "cherish me" through all my tribulations. "Upon my word, everything seems to be narrow where it ought to be broad, and the waist of this coat might be made for a hogshead;[3] and, ugh! this shirt collar is cutting my ears off, and you have not a decent cravat in the whole lot, and your vests are frights, and what am I to do with my hair?" Still no reply from Mr. Fern, who lay on the floor, faintly ejaculating,[4] between his fits of laughter, "Oh, my! by Jove! oh! by Jupiter!"

Was that to hinder me? Of course not. Strings and pins, women's never-failing resort, soon brought broadcloth and kerseymere[5] to terms. I parted my hair on one side, rolled it under, and then secured it with hair pins; chose the best fitting coat, and capping the climax with one of those soft, cozy hats, looked in the glass,[6] where I beheld the very facsimile of a certain musical gentleman, whose photograph hangs this minute in Brady's entry.[7]

Well, Mr. Fern seized his hat, and out we went together. "Fanny," said he, "you must not take my arm; you are a fellow." "True," said I. "I forgot; and you must not help me over the puddles, as you did just now, and do, for mercy's sake, stop laughing. There, there goes your hat—I mean *my* hat; confound the wind! and down comes my hair; lucky 'tis dark, isn't it?" But oh, the delicious freedom of that walk,

---

1   *Mr. Fern*   James Parton, whom Fern had married in 1856. She did not adopt his surname.

2   *Tailors*   I.e., sewers of men's rather than women's clothing.

3   *hogshead*   Large barrel.

4   *ejaculating*   Exclaiming.

5   *broadcloth*   Fine wool material often used in men's jackets;   *kerseymere*   Fine twill wool material.

6   *glass*   Mirror.

7   *a certain musical ... Brady's entry*   Fern is likely referring to her brother, the composer Richard Storrs Willis (1819–1900); "Brady" refers to the prominent New York-based photographer Mathew Brady (1822–96).

after we were well started! No skirts to hold up, or to draggle their wet folds against my ankles; no stifling veil flapping in my face, and blinding my eyes; no umbrella to turn inside out, but instead, the cool rain driving slap into my face, and the resurrectionized blood coursing through my veins, and tingling in my cheeks. To be sure, Mr. Fern occasionally loitered behind, and leaned up against the side of a house to enjoy a little private "guffaw," and I could now and then hear a gasping "Oh, Fanny! Oh, my!" but none of these things moved me, and if I don't have a nicely fitting suit of my own to wear rainy evenings, it is because—well, there *are* difficulties in the way. Who's the best tailor?

Now, if any male or female Miss Nancy[1] who reads this feels shocked, let 'em! Any woman who likes, may stay at home during a three weeks' rain, till her skin looks like parchment, and her eyes like those of a dead fish, or she may go out and get a consumption[2] dragging round wet petticoats; I won't—I positively declare I won't. I shall begin *evenings* when *that* suit is made, and take private walking lessons with Mr. Fern, and they who choose may crook their backs at home for fashion, and then send for the doctor to straighten them; I prefer to patronize my shoe-maker and tailor. I've as good a right to preserve the healthy body God gave me, as if I were not a woman.

—1858

---

1  *Miss Nancy*  Prudish individual.
2  *get a consumption*  Contract tuberculosis (or, more loosely, get sick).

# Independence

"Fourth of July." Well—I don't feel patriotic. Perhaps I might if they would stop that deafening racket. Washington was very well, if he *couldn't* spell, and I'm glad we are all free; but as a woman— I shouldn't know it, didn't some orator tell me. Can I go out of an evening without a hat[1] at my side? Can I go out with one on my head without danger of a station-house?[2] Can I clap my hands at some public speaker when I am nearly bursting with delight? Can I signify the contrary when my hair stands on end with vexation? Can I stand up in the cars "like a gentleman" without being immediately invited "to sit down"? Can I get into an omnibus[3] without having my sixpence taken from my hand and given to the driver? Can I cross Broadway without having a policeman tackled to my helpless elbow? Can I go to see anything *pleasant*, like an execution or a dissection? Can I drive that splendid "Lantern,"[4] distancing—like his owner—all competitors? Can I have the nomination for "Governor of Vermont," like our other contributor, John G. Saxe?[5] Can I be a Senator, that I may hurry up that millennial International Copyright Law?[6] Can I *even* be President? Bah—you know I can't. "*Free!*" Humph!

—1859

---

1   *a hat*   I.e., a man.

2   *Can I ... station-house?*   Many jurisdictions in America had laws against cross-dressing; Fern implies that she could not go out wearing a man's hat without fear of being arrested (as had happened to other women).

3   *omnibus*   Horse-drawn public carriage traveling a fixed route with set stops.

4   *Lantern*   Reference to a racing horse owned by *New York Ledger* editor Robert Bonner.

5   *John G. Saxe*   American poet (1816–87) who unsuccessfully ran for governor of Vermont in 1859, whose works were published in the *Ledger*.

6   *International Copyright Law*   Prior to the 1886 Berne Convention for the Protection of Literary and Artistic Works, American authors had little or no legal protection against their works being copied and republished abroad without the authors being compensated.

# The Working-Girls of New York

Nowhere more than in New York does the contest between squalor and splendor so sharply present itself. This is the first reflection of the observing stranger who walks its streets. Particularly is this noticeable with regard to its women. Jostling on the same pavement with the dainty fashionista is the care-worn working-girl. Looking at both these women, the question arises, which lives the more miserable life—she whom the world styles "fortunate," whose husband belongs to three clubs, and whose only meal with his family is an occasional breakfast, from year's end to year's end; who is as much a stranger to his own children as to the reader; whose young son of seventeen has already a detective on his track employed by his father to ascertain where and how he spends his nights and his father's money; swift retribution for that father who finds food, raiment, shelter, equipages[1] for his household; but love, sympathy, companionship—never? Or she—this other woman—with a heart quite as hungry and unappeased, who also faces day by day the same appalling question: *Is this all life has for me?*

A great book is yet unwritten about women. Michelet[2] has aired his wax-doll theories regarding them. The defender of "woman's rights" has given us her views. Authors and authoresses of little, and big repute, have expressed themselves on this subject, and none of them as yet have begun to grasp it: men—because they lack spirituality, rightly and justly to interpret women; women—because they dare not, or will not, tell us that which most interests us to know. Who shall write this bold, frank, truthful book remains to be seen. Meanwhile woman's millennium is yet a great way off; and while it slowly progresses, conservatism and indifference gaze through their spectacles at the seething elements of today, and wonder "what ails all our women?"

Let me tell you what ails the working-girls. While yet your breakfast is progressing, and your toilet unmade, comes forth through Chatham Street and the Bowery, a long procession of them by twos

---

1   *raiment*  Clothing;  *equipages*  Articles of fashionable life.
2   *Michelet*  French historian and social critic Jules Michelet (1798–1874), who characterized women as loving, childlike, and subservient.

and threes to their daily labor. Their breakfast, so called, has been hastily swallowed in a tenement house, where two of them share, in a small room, the same miserable bed. Of its quality you may better judge, when you know that each of these girls pays but three dollars a week for board, to the working man and his wife where they lodge.

The room they occupy is close and unventilated, with no accommodations for personal cleanliness, and so near to the little Flinegans[1] that their Celtic night-cries are distinctly heard. They have risen unrefreshed, as a matter of course, and their ill-cooked breakfast does not mend the matter. They emerge from the doorway where their passage is obstructed by "nanny goats" and ragged children rooting together in the dirt, and pass out into the street. They shiver as the sharp wind of early morning strikes their temples. There is no look of youth on their faces; hard lines appear there. Their brows are knit; their eyes are sunken; their dress is flimsy, and foolish, and tawdry; always a hat, and feather or soiled artificial flower upon it; a soiled petticoat; a greasy dress, a well-worn sacque[2] or shawl, and a gilt breastpin and earrings.

Now follow them to the large, black-looking building, where several hundred of them are manufacturing hoop-skirts.[3] If you are a woman you have worn plenty; but you little thought what passed in the heads of these girls as their busy fingers glazed the wire, or prepared the spools for covering them, or secured the tapes which held them in their places. *You* could not stay five minutes in that room, where the noise of the machinery used is so deafening, that only by the motion of the lips could you comprehend a person speaking.

Five minutes! Why, these young creatures bear it, from seven in the morning till six in the evening; week after week, month after month, with only half an hour at midday to eat their dinner of a slice of bread and butter or an apple, which they usually eat in the building, some of them having come a long distance. As I said, the roar of machinery in that room is like the roar of Niagara. Observe them as

---

1   *little Flinegans*   This made-up name suggests the degree to which such lower-income areas were inhabited by those of Irish descent. (*Flynn* and *Finnegan* are both common Irish names.)

2   *sacque*   Loose-fitting women's cloak or jacket.

3   *hoop-skirts*   Large, rigidly wired undergarments worn to provide the broad-skirted shape fashionable during the mid-nineteenth century.

you enter. Not one lifts her head. They might as well be machines, for any interest or curiosity they show, save always to know *what o'clock it is*. Pitiful! pitiful, you almost sob to yourself, as you look at these young girls. *Young?* Alas! it is only in years that they are young.

————

"Only three dollars a week do they earn," said I to a brawny woman in a tenement house near where some of them boarded. "Only three dollars a week, and all of that goes for their board. How, then, do they clothe themselves?" Hell has nothing more horrible than the cold, sneering indifference of her reply: "*Ask the dry-good men.*"[1]

Perhaps you ask, why do not these girls go out to service? Surely it were better to live in a clean, nice house, in a healthy atmosphere, with respectable people, who might take other interest in them than to wring out the last particle of their available bodily strength. It were better surely to live in a house cheerful and bright, where merry voices were sometimes heard, and clean, wholesome food was given them. Why do they not? First, because, unhappily, they look down upon the position of a servant, even from *their* miserable standpoint. But chiefly, and mainly, because when six o'clock in the evening comes they are their own mistresses, without hindrance or questioning, till another day of labor begins. They do not sit in an underground kitchen, watching the bell-wire,[2] and longing to see what is going on out of doors. More's the pity that the street is their only refuge from the squalor and quarrelling and confusion of their tenement-house home. More's the pity, that as yet there are no sufficiently decent, cleanly boarding houses, within their means, where their self-respect would not inevitably wither and die.

As it is, they stroll the streets; and who can blame them? *There* are gay lights, and fine shop windows. It costs nothing to *wish* they could have all those fine things. They look longingly into the theatres, through whose doors happier girls of their own age pass, radiant and smiling, with their lovers. Glimpses of Paradise come through those doors as they gaze. Back comes the old torturing question: Must my

---

1   *dry-good men*   Sellers of textiles and other household items. The implication appears to be that the women are driven into sex work in order to afford clothes.

2   *bell-wire*   In a wealthy person's house, various rooms were connected to the kitchen (and/or the servants' quarters) via a bell-pull system; one pulled a cord from whichever room one was in in order to summon a servant to that room.

young life *always* be toil? *nothing* but toil? They stroll on. Music and bright lights from the underground "Concert Saloons," where girls like themselves get fine dresses and good wages, and flattering words and smiles beside. Alas! the future is far away; the present only is tangible. Is it a wonder if they never go back to the dark, cheerless tenement-house, or to the "manufactory" which sets their poor, weary bodies aching, till they feel forsaken of God and man? Talk of virtue! Live this life of toil, and starvation, and friendlessness, and "unwomanly rags," and learn charity. Sometimes they rush for escape into ill-sorted marriages, with coarse rough fellows, and go back to the old tenement-house life again, with this difference, that their toil does *not* end at six o'clock, and that from *this* bargain there is no release but death.

But there are other establishments than those factories where working-girls are employed. There is "Madame ——, Modiste."[1] Surely the girls working there must fare better. Madame pays six thousand dollars rent for the elegant mansion in that fashionable street, in the basement or attic of which they work. Madame cuts and makes dresses, but she takes in none of the materials for that purpose.[2] Not she. She coolly tells you that she will make you a very nice *plain* black silk dress, and find everything, for two hundred dollars. This is modest, at a clear profit to herself of one hundred dollars on every such dress, particularly as she buys all her material by the wholesale, and pays her girls, at the highest rate of compensation, not more than six dollars a week. At this rate of small wages and big profits, you can well understand how she can afford not only to keep up this splendid establishment, but another still more magnificent for her own *private* residence in quite as fashionable a neighborhood. Another "modiste" who *did* "take in material for dresses," and—ladies also! was in the habit of telling the latter that thirty-two yards of any material was required where sixteen would have answered. The remaining yards were then in all cases thrown into a rag-pen; from which, through contract with a man in her employ, she furnished herself with all the crockery, china, glass, tin and iron ware needed in her household. This same modiste employed twenty-five girls at the starvation price

---

1   *Modiste*   Fashionable seamstress.

2   *takes in … that purpose*   I.e., she will supply the materials herself, as opposed to accepting materials supplied by the client, as was more common at the time.

of three dollars and a half a week. The room in which they worked was about nine feet square, with only one window in it, and whoso came early enough to secure a seat by that window saved her eyesight by the process. Three sewing-machines whirred constantly by day in this little room, which at night was used as a sleeping apartment. As the twenty-five working-girls were ushered in to their day's labor in the morning before that room was ventilated, you would not wonder that by four in the afternoon dark circles appeared under their eyes, and they stopped occasionally to press their hands upon their aching temples. Not often, but *sometimes*, when the pain and exhaustion became intolerable.

One of the twenty-five was an orphan girl named Lizzy, only fifteen years of age. Not even this daily martyrdom had quenched her abounding spirits, in that room where never a smile was seen on another face—where never a jest was ventured on, not even when Madame's back was turned. Always Lizzie's hair was nicely smoothed, and though the clean little creature went without her breakfast—for a deduction of wages was the penalty of being late—yet had she always on a clean dark calico dress, smoothed by her own deft little fingers. In that dismal, smileless room she was the only sunbeam. But one day the twenty-five were startled; their needles dropped from their fingers. Lizzie was worn out at last! Her pretty face blanched, and with a low baby cry she threw her arms over her face and sobbed: "Oh, I *cannot* bear this life—I cannot bear it any longer. George *must* come and take me away from this." That night she was privately married to "George," who was an employee on the railroad. The next day while on the train attending to his duties, he broke his arm, and neither of the bridal pair having any money, George was taken to the hospital. The little bride, with starvation before her, went back that day to Madame, and concealing the fact of her marriage, begged humbly to be taken back, apologizing for her conduct on the day before, on the plea that she had such a violent pain in her temples that she knew not what she said. As she was a handy little workwoman, her request was granted, and she worked there for several weeks, during her honeymoon, at the old rate of pay. The day George was pronounced well, she threw down her work, clapped her little palms together, and announced to the astonished twenty-five that they had a married woman among them, and that she should not return the next morning. Being the middle of the week, and not the end, she had to go without her wages for that week. Romance was not part or parcel of Madame's establishment. Her law was as the Medes and Persians,[1] which changed not. Little Lizzie's future was no more to her than her past had been—no more than that of another young thing in that workroom, who begged a friend, each day, to bring her ever so little ardent spirits,[2] at the half hour allotted to their miserable dinner, lest she should fail in strength to finish the day's work, upon which so much depended.

Oh! if the ladies who wore the gay robes manufactured in that room knew the tragedy of those young lives, would they not be to them like the penance robes of which we read, piercing, burning, torturing?

There is still another class of girls, who tend in the large shops in New York. Are they not better remunerated and lodged? We shall see. The additional dollar or two added to their wages is offset by the necessity of their being always nicely apparelled, and the necessity of a better lodging house, and consequently a higher price for board, so that unless they are fortunate enough to have a parent's roof over their heads, they will not, except in rare cases, where there is a special gift as an accountant, or an artist-touch in the fingers, to twist a ribbon or frill a lace, be able to save any more than the class of which I have been speaking. They are allowed, however, by their employers, to purchase any article in the store at first cost,[3] which is something in their favor.

But, you say, is there no bright side to this dark picture? Are there no cases in which these girls battle bravely with penury?[4] I have one in my mind now; a girl, I should say a lady; one of nature's ladies, with a face as refined and delicate as that of any lady who bends over these pages; who has been through this harrowing experience of the working-girl, and after years of patience, virtuous toil, has no more at this day than when she began, i.e., her wages day by day. Of the wretched places she has called "home," I will not pain you by speaking. Of the rough words she has borne, that she was powerless,

---

1   *as the Medes and Persians*   See Daniel 6.12: "The thing is true, according to the law of the Medes and Persians, which altereth not."

2   *ardent spirits*   Strong alcohol.

3   *first cost*   I.e., the base cost of an item, not marked up for profit.

4   *penury*   Poverty.

through her poverty, to resent. Of the long walks she has taken to obtain wages due, and failed to secure them at last. Of the weary, wakeful nights, and heart-breaking days, borne with a heroism and trust in God, that was truly sublime. Of the little remittances from time to time forwarded to old age and penury, in "the old country," when she herself was in want of comfortable clothing; when she herself had no shelter in case of sickness, save the hospital or the almshouse. Surely, such virtue and integrity will have more enduring record than in these pages.

Humanity has not slept on this subject, though it has as yet accomplished little. A boarding house has been established in New York for working-girls, excellent in its way, but intended mainly for those who "have seen better days," and not for the most needy class of which I have spoken. A noble institution, however, called "The Working Woman's Protective Union," has sprung up, for the benefit of this latter class, their object being to find places *in the country*, for such of these girls as will leave the overcrowded city, not as servants, but as operatives on sewing machines, and to other similar revenues of employment. Their places are secured before they are sent. The person who engages them pays their expenses on leaving, and the consent of parents, or guardians, or friends, is always obtained before they leave. A room is to be connected with this institution, containing several sewing machines, where gratuitous instruction will be furnished to those who desire it. A lawyer of New York has generously volunteered his services also, to collect the too-tardy wages of these girls, due from flinty-hearted employers. Many of the girls who have applied here are under fifteen. At first, they utterly refused to go into the country, which to them was only another name for dullness; even preferring to wander up and down the streets of the city, half-fed and half-clothed, in search of employment, than to leave its dear kaleidoscopic delights. But after a little, when letters came from some who had gone; the wages that one could live and save money on; their kind treatment; the good, wholesome food and fresh air; their hearty, jolly country fun; and more than all, when it was announced that one of their number had actually married an ex-governor, the matter took another aspect. And, though all may not marry governors, and some may not marry at all, it still remains that *inducing them to go to the country is striking a brave blow at the root of the evil*; for we all know that human strength and human virtue have their limits; and the dreadful pressure of temptations and present ease, upon the discouragement, poverty and friendlessness of the working-girls of New York, must be gratifying to the devil. I do not hesitate to say, that there is no institution of the present day, more worthy to be sustained, or that more imperatively challenges the good works and good wishes of the benevolent, than "The New York Working Woman's Protective Union." May God speed it!

—1868

# In Context

## Contemporary Reviews of Fanny Fern's Work

Fanny Fern's rapid rise to fame and wealth during the early 1850s led to substantial discussion among journalists and literary critics. The 6 May 1854 issue of *The Musical World and New York Musical Times*, for which Fern wrote regularly and whose editor had helped publish her first two collections, included a full-page spread excerpting laudatory reviews of her work from numerous contemporary newspapers, including from influential papers such as *Harper's Magazine* and *Godey's Lady's Book*.

## $15,000 THE FIRST YEAR, IS A PRETTY FAIR SUM FOR AN AUTHOR TO MAKE!!

Fanny Fern's popularity is still on the increase; the sale of her works continues unprecedented; it is with difficulty that the demand can be supplied. The secret of this success is perhaps hinted at in the subjoined notices of her works, which are selected at random from a peck or so now on our table. First, comes the opinion of that leviathan of literature, *Harper's Magazine.*

> A second series of *Fern Leaves from Fanny's Portfolio* is published by Miller, Orton & Mulligan, which in many respects is superior to the former quaint and merry productions which have procured such a sudden access of fame to the lively authoress. Usually, we have little faith in these rapid growths of popularity. The temple of fame is not to be taken by storm, but must be approached by steep and winding ways. A desperate rush is apt to defeat itself. But Fanny Fern doubtless forms an exception to this rule. The favor with which her writings have been received—almost unprecedented in this country and in England—has a legitimate cause. She dips her pen in her heart, and writes out her own feelings and fancies. She is no imitator,

no dealer in second-hand wares. Her inspiration comes from nature, not from books. She dares to be original. She has no fear of critics or of the public before her eyes. She conquers a peace with them by sheer force of audacity. Often verging on the bounds of wholesome conventionalities, she still shows a true and kindly nature—she has always the sympathy with suffering which marks the genuine woman—and her most petulant and frolicksome moods are softened by a perennial vein of tender humaneness. Fanny Fern is a poetess, though she avoids the use of rhyme. With all her sense of the ludicrous, she knows how to seize the poetical aspects of life, and these are rendered in picturesque and melodious phrase, which lacks nothing but rhythm to be true poetry. Her rapid transitions from fun to pathos are very effective. Her pictures of domestic life, in its multiform relations, are so faithful to nature as to excite alternate smiles and tears. We regard her extraordinary success as a good omen. She has won her way unmistakably to the hearts of the people; and this we interpret as a triumph of natural feeling. It shows that the day for stilted rhetoric, scholastic refinements, and big dictionary words, the parade, pomp, and pageantry of literature, is declining; and that the writer who is brave enough to build on universal human sympathies, is sure of the most grateful reward in unaffected popular appreciation.—*Harper's Magazine.*

Miss Swisshelm[1] on Fanny Fern.—Miss Swisshelm, the able and conscientious editress of the *Pittsburgh Saturday Visitor,* who is so hard to please, so independent, so unflinchingly honest and bold in her utterance, thus discourses on the characteristics of "Our Fanny": "Fanny Fern is a genius, and one who has told the world a great deal of wholesome truth which that same world very much needed to hear: truth that, like the good seed, will bring forth good fruits in their season. Very grave objections are made to Fanny's style, in that it is not always according to Lindlay Murray;[2] but one thing is certain; Fanny's language answers

---

1   *Miss Swisshelm*   Journalist and women's rights activist Jane Swisshelm (1815–84).

2   *Lindlay Murray*   American grammarian best known for his widely adopted schoolbooks on grammar (1745–1826).

the original intent of that commodity, for it does convey ideas, and unlike many polished sentences, leaves no doubt as to the idea it was intended to convey. Fanny has a rare good gift of telling in a few words what she thinks, and thinking a great many times, something well worthy of being told. Her sentiment is no sham, for its utterance has that unmistakable sign of feeling, the power to awake an answering chord in other hearts. Her pages are more like bunches of mignonette[1] than leaves of fern, for they are generally better than at first glance one might suppose—and under a plain, simple garb exhale a rare odor. To us they look like an amiable, beautiful and polished woman dressed in peasant's homespun—they exhibit the deep and exquisite sensibility draped in plain, homely common sense; and to us her scraps are more refreshing, especially after some of the more elaborate compositions which afflict the public, and in which, or rather *on* which, sensibility spread as a varnish, is quite unable to hide selfishness within. Fanny is always talking about herself, but never conveys an idea of egotism—she never obtrudes herself between you and the picture she presents for your inspection, but stands at your side and points it out. We do like Fanny for her genial temper, and for retaining the milk of human kindness in her heart, sweet and fresh through reverses of fortune, disappointments and troubles, which would have turned a common nature into vinegar. Her reproofs are often pungent but never sour or bitter. They often have a horse-radishy flavor, but never taste of wormwood, henbane or gall;[2] and when she probes a wound, it is never with a poisoned arrow.—*Pittsburgh Sat. Visitor.*

Fanny Fern and Eliza Cook[3] are sister spirits. Although Eliza is more *ver*satile, Fanny, having enjoyed the birthright of freedom, possesses wilder spirits. She is the buxom nymph of sylvan shades and sunny nooks; she shoots her fiery darts at random, but they always hit the mark. Fern leaves, like the Chinese sensitive leaves, are magical tests of character—they sympathize only

---

1   *mignonette*  Herbaceous plant with small, unassuming flowers and a strong fragrance.
2   *wormwood, henbane or gall*  Bitter-tasting plants and substances.
3   *Eliza Cook*  English poet known for her advocacy for women's rights (1818–89).

with congenial spirits; therefore Fanny may felicitate herself with this pleasurable assurance, that her reciprocating friends are as innumerable as the enchanted leaves she has scattered over the two hemispheres. Fanny's Portfolio is like the wizard's—it contains a charm for everybody.—*N. Y. Mercantile Guide.*

FERN LEAVES SECOND SERIES.—We welcome another volume of Fern Leaves. Where in the world are our male authors? To arms! authors who wear the unmentionables![1] The laurels are sliding from your brows! The best and most readable books are being written by women! You are a bold operator "Fanny," and we like you the better for it. There is no Homeopathy about you! no mixing, no diluting and dosing. But have a care, "Fanny"! It is not every case that will bear your knife and caustic; for if you use them too unsparingly, you will kill as well as cure. There are some natures made of such contradictory stuff, that the more you chasten them, the more hardened they become; yet speak to them a soft and gentle word, persuade instead of deriding, and they will fall at your feet. The second series of Fern Leaves consists of 120 short articles, much resembling our author's first work under the same title published last summer. They are written with much spirit and sprightliness, and her woman's heart is seen through all nobly striving to denounce sin, and defend virtue, wherever found.—*Iowa Journal of Education.*

No writer in our country has ever, in so short a period, gained an equal celebrity, or touched so many of the heartstrings of the million. Keen, satirical, probing to the very depths of conventional wrongs; pricking the consciences of delinquent husbands, and scathing wayward wives and mothers; entering humble households, sympathising with all her womanly nature with human suffering, she has gone out from them and lashed with an unsparing hand the tyrannies of social life; she has been among the "upper ten" and the "lower millions," with no tongue of flattery for the faults of either; and yet all have fallen in with the gentle and kindly current of her thoughts. Blessings upon

---

1    *unmentionables*    In this context, trousers.

the head of Fanny Fern! and may she continue to pluck "leaves" that have so much moral fragrance. This new series is dedicated to a Lockport "boy," or MAN we will call him, for his years now, and more than all, his praiseworthy self-elevation, well entitles him to all the prerogatives of manhood. Who would not be proud of such a dedication from such a source? "To my truest friend, Oliver Dyer,[1] whose friendship never faltered in adversity; whose sympathy and encouragement cheered me when no bow of promise was set in my sky, this book is gratefully dedicated."—*Niagara Democrat*.

The success of Fanny Fern as a writer is one of the curiosities and marvels of literature. And yet it is all natural enough. She is an original and brilliant writer, and combines all those qualities which make up a formidable reputation—such as she now enjoys. Her Leaves contain passages that are witty, pathetic, satirical and also much that is genial and full of heart. If she is severe, it is only to rebuke some wrong, and if the dart of satire is thrown, it is merited. There is no malice, but rather justice in her writings. She seems to have all the flow of Irving, the polish of "Ike Marvel," and the edge of Dickens.[2] In style she has nothing stiff or awkward, any more than she has in conversation. She writes like one who feels with intensity, whether she means to put roses or thorns into the mental heart. With a nice eye to the real or the sham, to those who seem and to those who *are*, to merit or pretence, she deals with discrimination and effect. We know of no writer who writes with such a heart; who puts the very vim[3] into the inkstand and upon paper. Always vivacious, earnest, energetic, she gives the public nothing that is not worth reading once, twice, and as many more times as a good thing is relished. Let all who wish for a work that will charm and improve, get this Second Series of Fern Leaves.—*Boston Bee*.

---

1   *Oliver Dyer*   Journalist and editor who had offered Fern her first contract as a columnist for the *Musical World and Times* in 1852.

2   *Irving*   American author Washington Irving (1783–1859), best known for his short fiction; *Ike Marvel*   Pen name (usually given as "Ik") of American author Donald Grant Mitchell (1822–1908);   *Dickens*   English novelist Charles Dickens (1812–70).

3   *vim*   Vigor.

Another book from Fanny Fern! Yes, and another yet, if she continues to write as gracefully and prettily as she has been doing. Little did we think some years ago—we won't name the time—when we first saw Fanny's golden locks fluttering in the breeze on Boston Common, that she would stir up such a sensation in the hearts of the people. Why, she has already written the most pleasing and popular book of the day, the copies selling by tens of thousands; and here she must come out with another, to tempt our affections and our purses. We make it a point to read everything of Fanny's that our eyes greet, and we never yet failed to glean the most delectable pleasure from her pages.—*N.Y. Atlas.*

Everyone—that is everyone in the habit of reading the newspapers—has read, and consequently admired at least a few of the long and short essays, paragraphs, and memorable remarks which, like flashing meteors, have shot athwart the literary firmament from time to time, to the amazement, in particular, of a certain class of quiet writers, who for a time have been left to wander in the gloom of the past. But, unlike meteors, which fade away after a brief flash, Fanny's flashes are designed for preservation, and are carefully collected together, and made to form a brilliant galaxy for permanent usefulness and lasting admiration. Her originality, industry and proficiency in all the departments of life and human knowledge, are wonderful, indeed, and therefore wonderfully widespread is her popularity. She is, besides, very bold and independent in her strictures on men, women, and every object else that comes in her way, and she has courage to say things which almost any common thinker might think, but which very few, perhaps, could put upon paper in the same nervous and striking language. Hence, no doubt, in a great measure, Fanny's popularity with the multitude of readers.—*Godey's Lady's Book.*

The secret of her power over the public mind, we apprehend, is that she has a heart. Gifted with noble faculties by nature, and mellowed, if rumor says truly, by the furnace of affliction, she has come out of her trials, or we may say, forced her way out by her own indomitable courage—refined and quickened, instead of imbruted and deadened; and now pours forth from the rich fountain of her experience, with the ardor and sincerity of a child, the rich stores she had garnered there. In addition, she has point and wit, and of course is always on the side of humanity and justice, and in warm sympathy with the poor and the oppressed. That such a writer, with works made up of detached sketches, should have achieved the popularity she has, is a fragrant indication that the heart of humanity is budding, and, indeed, about to bloom.—*N.Y. Universe.*

Fanny is a genius, bright, sparkling, witty, racy and sensible withal. There is a vein of common sense underlying all her sarcasm, which makes her writings subservient to good morals and integrity. We trust her Leaves are for the cure of some follies, as well as instructive and amusing.—*Maine Farmer.*

Fern Leaves—Second Series—Fanny Fern's spicy, lively, heart-spoken productions, are most agreeable and racy specimens of composition. Everybody should read them, for everybody must enjoy their perusal.—*Utica Observer.*

# *Fern Leaves* and *Leaves of Grass*

As she made clear in her laudatory 1856 review of *Leaves of Grass* (excerpted earlier in this volume), Fanny Fern was an enthusiastic supporter of the poet Walt Whitman and his fresh, free, and innovative poetics—and the admiration went both ways. When Whitman conceived of the cover design for the first edition of *Leaves of Grass*, he clearly took inspiration from Fern's recent prose bestseller, *Fern Leaves from Fanny's Portfolio*, with its deep green binding, lavish gold embossing, and botanically inspired typeface. Contemporary reviewers were alert to the connections between Fern's prose and Whitman's verse: a critic for the London-based *Punch Magazine* asserted that Whitman's volume was "fully worthy to be put on a level with that heap of rubbish called *Fern Leaves*, by Fanny Fern, and similarly 'green stuff.'"

Front cover of *Fern Leaves from Fanny's Portfolio* (1853).

Front cover of the first edition of *Leaves of Grass* (1855).

## From the Publisher

A name never says it all, but the word "Broadview" expresses a good deal of the philosophy behind our company. We are open to a broad range of academic approaches and political viewpoints. We pay attention to the broad impact book publishing and book printing has in the wider world; for some years now we have used 100% recycled paper for most titles. Our publishing program is internationally oriented and broad-ranging. Our individual titles often appeal to a broad readership too; many are of interest as much to general readers as to academics and students.

Founded in 1985, Broadview remains a fully independent company owned by its shareholders—not an imprint or subsidiary of a larger multinational.

To order our books or obtain up-to-date information, please visit broadviewpress.com.

broadview press
www.broadviewpress.com

This book is made of paper from well-managed FSC® - certified
forests, recycled materials, and other controlled sources.